STAR QUEST
BOOKS
VOLUME 2

Operation
Master
Planet

STAR QUEST BOOKS

VOLUME 2

Operation Master Planet

GREGORY J. SMITH

BETHANY HOUSE PUBLISHERS

MINNEAPOLIS, MINNESOTA 55438

A Division of Bethany Fellowship, Inc.

GREGORY JON SMITH, a sci-fi buff since his teen years, has combined his love for the genre with his skill as a professional writer. A graduate from the University of Minnesota, he worked as the publications director for Lutherans for Life for a number of years, has written several articles for community newspapers and has been a contributing editor to *Debate* magazine. He presently works at Lutheran Brotherhood as a financial paraplanner. *Operation Master Planet* is the sequel to *Captive Planet*.

Copyright © 1986
Gregory J. Smith
All Rights Reserved

Published by Bethany House Publishers
A Division of Bethany Fellowship, Inc.
6820 Auto Club Road, Minneapolis, Minnesota 55438

Printed in the United States of America

Library of Congress Cataloging-in-Publication Data

Smith, Gregory J. (Gregory Jon)
    Operation master planet.

    (Star quest books ; v. 2)
    I. Title.   II. Series.
PS3569.M535706   1986   813'.54   86-26882
ISBN 0-87123-673-7 (pbk.)

To the unwanted and imperfect,
both born and unborn—
because you *are*.

Chapter One

Lam Laeo turned sharply, his attention riveted behind him. Except for the stars, two of Neece's tiny moons alone illuminated the road, and Lam's eyes strained through the darkness, alert for movement. All he could see were the fernlike trees bending over the road, waving in the breeze as if to urge him forward.

"Did you hear something?" Lam asked the attractive young woman beside him.

"You mean something besides the nightly insect riot?" Lista asked.

Lam listened again for a moment, but he could hear only tree leaves sweeping the air and the tumultuous chirping, croaking night life.

"Forget it," Lam said. He tugged gently on Lista's arm and they resumed their trek to town, eager to reach their rooms at the inn.

The two of them had left the restoration camp before sunset, and Lam was looking forward to a peaceful walk back to New Highland, Neece's spaceport town. Laden with forest scents, the refreshing air gusted around them, gently tossing their hair. Lam enjoyed Neece's lush, wild beauty—and he enjoyed Lista's company.

Everything seemed right for a pleasant evening. But there was something else—an unsettling feeling. Lam gazed at Lista's profile outlined in the moonlight. *She's trying to cover it*, he thought, *but she feels uncomfortable, too.*

The sound reached them again—a rustling that seemed out of rhythm with the breeze, a footfall too heavy to belong to any creature of the planet. But Lam had looked back several times already, and he was determined not to give in to his nerves again.

It could have been a night feeder, one of the large birds that hunted at sunset. Their dark blue bodies and large, powerful wings were strong enough to disturb the forest that bordered both sides of the road. Or it could have been one or more of the furry little tree-dwellers on which the birds preyed, startled by the two-legged trespassers into their territory.

But Lista, too, seemed increasingly anxious. She had been on the planet much longer than Lam, and she should know better than he if they were simply succumbing to a childish fear of the dark, seeing beasts lurking in every shadow. Her anxiety confirmed Lam's own apprehensions.

Then a shrill cry from the forest on Lista's side tore through the night, and a panicked bird flapped from its leafy cover and escaped into the star-sprayed sky.

"Lista, run!" Lam yelled, but his warning came too late. The same instant he saw two shadows lunge at Lista; an attacker from the woods on his side grabbed him and twisted his arms back while another punched his fist into Lam's stomach. He slumped to the gravel, gasping for breath.

"Some people have been disturbed by your questions," hissed a shadow looming above him. "Forget the old man and worry about yourself."

Lam lay heaving and squinting into the darkness. He could just make out three men in dark clothing, their faces hidden.

"And if you rile up your native pals, you'll get the same treatment they're going to get," the spokesman warned. "They're lazy fools who don't care what happens to anyone. Stay away from them!"

"Give him something more to help him remember what he's learned," another shadowy figure commanded.

Lam heard shuffling in the pebbles and dimly saw a boot driving toward his head. Before he could move, it struck him and he sank in a swirling pool of color and confused noise.

In his mind, the colors flowed together into a sun, into foliage, into a scene of broken pavement. Grass and wild flowers strained their way up between the cracks in the pavement and rippled in the breeze. The noise began to sound like a familiar voice.

"Lam, I've been looking for you," the voice called out. The voice belonged to Hud, the acting presider of the planet Tsu's Royal Council, but the events his mind was reliving were, in both time and distance, far from his body.

The day was the kind that made a person want to work. It was fairly bright—Tsu's constant cloud cover was thin that morning—and a cool breeze refreshed the workers as they toiled. Lam loaded the last of the rubble into a cart, pulled a towel from his pocket, and wiped off the sweat that threatened to roll into his eyes. As he leaned backward to stretch his sore muscles, a skip sped away, pulling the cart of rubble behind it.

"Good morning!" *Hud walked toward Lam across the fragmented pavement, his light blue robe fluttering behind him.*

"Good morning," *Lam replied cheerfully, wiping the dust from his face and hands.* "The work is going well. We have the whole south side of the city nearly cleaned up. The rebuilding can begin soon."

"Good. The sooner we can put the destruction of the Dominion behind us, the better."

Lam watched his friend gaze about the ruined city, remembering the stunned looks on the Tsuians faces when they returned from exile. The Dominion, under Kurdon, had devastated the beautiful cities on Tsu; nothing but rubble remained of the palace city with its spaceport, colorful markets, and the palace itself. The sadness in Hud's gentle eyes told Lam how painful it was to remember the city's past splendor.

Lam knew how the Tsuians felt; he had received an even deeper wound on his home planet, Entar. Returning from a merchant apprenticeship, he found that the Dominion had made an example of Entar. Nothing survived; lifeless ruins and scars marked the earth and Lam's memory.

"Did you want something?" *asked Lam, breaking Hud from his reverie.*

"Yes, Lam." *Hud turned his brown-green eyes back to Lam.* "You know that the Council refuses to send a non-Tsuian as an ambassador, but you've been a part of us for a long time, and we trust both your faith and your abilities."

"So?" *Lam questioned. Hud raised a tanned arm to shield his eyes from the sun as he spoke to Lam.*

"Tell me honestly how you have been feeling lately. You went *through quite an ordeal against the Dominion—and that was less than a year ago."*

"You're just like your brother Padu used to be. Why don't you just tell me what you want?"

Hud chuckled at Lam's frankness.

"Very well. Several years before the Dominion, the Royal Council sent an ambassador named Altua to a planet called Neece."

"I don't think I know it."

"You've probably heard of its sister planet, Vassir."

"Yes. That's where most of the Redlyn in my ship came from."

"Altua was our representative to both Neece and Vassir, but we have not heard from him since the Dominion conquered the system."

"Was he killed?" Lam asked.

"We don't think so. We contacted the authorities on both planets, and they reported that he was last living on Neece, but has not been seen for some time. They say he may have been captured by the native race on Neece."

"But you don't think so."

"Let me finish my story. When the Dominion fell, the governor of Neece killed himself because he had co-operated with the Dominion and carried out dozens of executions for them. According to the stories I've heard, which were several months old by the time I heard them, the governor on Vassir, a man named Kruge, managed to stay in control and pull together some sort of global government. He is more respectable than Neece's late governor, but I understand his character is still somewhat suspect."

"You still haven't told me what you want."

"You usually tell me what I want," grinned Hud.

Lam gave Hud half a smile. "When do you want me to leave?"

"Don't be so eager. Altua is a wise man, and strong in the Way of Tsu. He wouldn't disappear unless there was some . . . trouble."

Lam turned the proposition over in his mind. It was not the mission he had hoped for—he wanted to be an ambassador and teach about the Way of Tsu. Still, it would be a challenge, and he would still be representing his adopted home planet. The risk wasn't a factor. Lam figured that if he could defeat the Dominion, he could find an ambassador.

"When would you like an answer?" Lam rephrased his question.

Hud replied with a confident smile, "This evening if possible. We can help you equip Starjumper, and you can leave tomorrow."

Lam squinted at the sun to get an idea how late in the day it was. He rubbed the back of his hand across his warm, moist forehead. He looked at his hand; it glistened not with sweat but with blood.

Blood? How did I get blood on my forehead? He started up, then fell back with pain, and remembered—he was not on Tsu; he was on Neece, and he lay in agony on the street.

"Lam!" a voice next to him called. "Lam! How badly are you hurt?"

"Lista?" Lam managed to gasp.

"You'll be well," her soothing voice assured. Lam thought that something in her voice sounded shaken. *Still,* Lam told himself, *Lista knows what she is doing. I will be well.*

"They did not hurt me much," Lista whispered as she felt for broken bones in Lam's fallen body. Her touch felt good, a healing touch. Another wave of pain swept over him and he gritted his teeth. More lights flashed behind his eyes and he passed out again.

Lista's healing hands stayed in his mind, and he seemed to see them again, this time working her hands over a child's swollen limb as a worried mother looked on.

"When did she hurt her leg?" Lista asked the mother, but the fretting woman did not understand her. Lista was from the developed planet of Vassir, a distant planet in space and culture from the simple ways and forest language of the Be'Nay, the native people of Neece. The mother turned to the young Be'Nay man beside her who acted as interpreter, a tall athletic man with dark skin and flashing eyes.

"Ten days ago," translated the young man. "We treated her right away, but the bones did not set and her leg began to swell."

"I have a great deal of respect for your ways, Me'Ben," said Lista to the young man, still probing the scared little girl's leg. "But she has an infection, and the only thing that will help now is this restorative."

Lista worked swiftly to administer the life-saving drug. The girl whimpered a bit, startled at the sound of the injection gun.

"Me'Ben," began Lista, "please see that she returns again in a couple of days for another injection." The strong young native tipped his head to show that he understood. A leather band kept his shoulder-length black hair in place. Lista turned her face to the sky and could feel

that the sun's rays were getting weak.

"Are there any other urgent problems?" asked Lista wearily.

"The others can wait, Mesha," replied Me'Ben, using the title of respect for single women among his people. Me'Ben announced the end of the day to those who had come to Lista's restoration camp on the outskirts of New Highland, the port town.

Lista wiped off her metal instruments and began to repack them in her bag. Lam sat nearby, waiting for a chance to speak with her. He had met Lista briefly at the inn where they both had rooms. He thought she might know something about Altua, and could tell her about the Be'Nay. He was anxious to find out whether they might have had anything to do with Altua's disappearance. As she packed up, she spoke quietly to Lam.

"These people don't need much. The bounty of the land feeds and protects them well," stated Lista reverently. "But every once in a while, a person needs antibiotics, or surgery." Lam nodded that he understood.

"If you're nodding, or looking confused, I can't tell," Lista scolded.

"I'm sorry," Lam repented. "It's easy to forget that you're—not sighted."

"Blind," she corrected matter-of-factly.

"You say you are looking for Altua?"

"Can you tell me anything about him?"

"Altua was, I mean is, a dear man. I came to Neece as a Restorer for the settlement, but Altua told me about the Be'Nay, and I've been spending most of my time out here. He also tried to tell me about some belief he had in the Source and Power, but we didn't have much time to talk about it before he left."

"Left for where?"

"He didn't say, but he said he would be gone only a few days— that was quite a while ago now, as you know."

"But you can help me look for him?"

"I'm not very much help in looking," jibed Lista. Lam was instantly embarrassed, and laughed with her uneasily. Her short, wavy auburn hair seemed to glow like embers in the red light of the setting sun. As the wind blew gently into their lean-to clinic, it tossed her hair in a moving frame about the soft features of her face. Her rugged canvas jacket and pants tucked into her laced-up suede boots provided a curious contrast to her delicate build. Her golden eyes were only pretty deco-

rations for her face—she was completely blind.

A thin metal band called a "finder" circled her head like a crown, making her look like a misplaced princess. The rare instruments were made in her home village of Travalia for those who, like Lista, were without sight. The silver circlets sent out waves of ultrasonic sound, then processed and communicated return vibrations to the wearer. It took years to learn how to interpret all the subtle signals of distance and density, but even without practice, a wearer could locate an object as if it were making a sound of its own.

And her voice, mused Lam, *friendly but stern—and a little bit shy. But what is it? There's something wrong with her voice now.*

"Lam!" Lista sobbed as she lifted his head from the gravel. "Can you hear me?"

"Lista?" groaned Lam. "Are you okay?"

"They just threw me around a little. Can you walk if I help?"

Lam tried flexing his arm muscles, then his leg muscles.

"It'd be easier if you held the world still," Lam complained. "I'll just have to try standing first."

"Move slowly," urged Lista. "I'm sure you have a concussion."

Lam felt Lista's gentle hands slip under his arms to support him as he stood. At times in the past couple of weeks he had wondered what it would be like if she put her arms around him, but he certainly wished there was a different reason for her embrace. He slowly pushed himself up from the stones, but they slipped under his hands. As he struggled to rise, the stars began to rearrange themselves and he sank back to the road.

"Move slowly," Lista reprimanded. After the dizziness passed, a different wave swept over him: Anger. *How dare those thugs do this to us!* Lam raged inwardly. He drew a sharp breath as his wounded ribs shot him a warning. *As soon as I can walk, I'm getting my pistol from Starjumper,* he swore to himself. *If those slime-eaters ever try something like this again . . .*

"Lam, can you walk if I help you?" whispered Lista into his ear as she bent over to help support him. Lam groaned that he could, but his eyes were shut tight from the throbbing in his head.

Lista could tell that Lam was not going to be much help in

finding their way back to town, so she adjusted her finder and scanned their surroundings. The delicate metallic circlet around her head reflected the dim light of the moon and stars when she turned her head one way and then the other, to receive detailed information about the objects in her surroundings.

"Come," Lista urged when she had determined the way to town and slung her restoration satchel over her shoulder.

A colorful but unorganized procession was underway as delegates from every nation on Vassir, wearing their national costumes, emerged from the Council chambers. The usual boisterous debate and good humor were replaced that evening with more hushed discussions.

Lassen NaRedlander tugged on the hem of his shirt. A belt of metal links set with Redlyn crystals normally held the loose top in place around his waist, but the day-long meeting had taken a toll on his appearance. The shiny fabric of his baggy pants was creased from hours of sitting, and he longed to unlace and kick off his ankle-high brown boots. He walked wearily from the chamber and stepped into the hall. Like the rest of the government center, the hallway was spacious and well kept. The simple tile floors were clean and the stone walls were polished. The ornate crystal lights suspended from the ceiling were mercifully dim, and Lassen rubbed his eyes as they adjusted to the more comfortable level.

At regular intervals along the wall hung deep red banners, each one with the black outline of a six-pointed star superimposed by two spheres, one sphere overlapping the other.

Lassen lounged between two banners, relieved that he could let his mind wander to thoughts less weighty than the ones they wrestled with earlier. Someone touched his arm—a teenaged boy dressed in the simple woven uniform of the government center servants. The style was distinctly Highland—the tunic was fur-lined and hung just below his waist. A knife was sheathed on the inside of his left boot, and a belt of woven leather with an antler buckle gathered his tunic. Like many Highland boys, his buckle bore a carving of the mountains that surrounded Wyntir, the capital of Highland and home of the government center.

"Greetings from Redland, Keneche Krugson," Lassen said rather formally.

"Highland welcomes you, sir," replied Keneche with a slight bow.

"What brings you here?" Lassen inquired, trying to hide his weariness, though his voice betrayed him anyway.

"It is my job to see to the needs of the delegates," replied Keneche with a smile. Something in the way he said it told Lassen that Keneche meant that his job was only an excuse for being there.

"My need is to sleep for several days," said Lassen, stifling a yawn.

"It was a long meeting," Keneche sympathized.

"There are many difficult issues facing our troubled planet, Vassir," explained Lassen, although Vassir's troubles did not need explaining.

"And our sister planet, Neece," added Keneche. Lassen turned his head and looked into Keneche's blue eyes. *There is definitely something behind them*, Lassen thought.

"Yes, and our sister planet," he agreed.

"You probably discussed Neece," said Keneche quietly.

"Along with many other things," answered Lassen, curious about the conversation he was having with one of Chairman Kruge's sons.

"The famine, the trouble in the government, the rumors of possible foreign invasion . . ." Keneche began listing the planet's ills.

"It sounds like you were listening in," Lassen observed, wondering at the young man's knowledge of the issues discussed.

"I am a son of the Chairman," Keneche pointed out. "My mother is not one of his favored wives now, and so I run errands instead of government. But I'm not without ears—or influence."

Lassen nodded his understanding. He had met Keneche once before and had been impressed by his efficiency and maturity. Lassen tried to look beyond Keneche's red hair, cut short on one side in a strange style popular with the Highland youth. He ignored the downy attempt at a moustache and the occasional teenage blemish and realized there was a serious underlying purpose behind Keneche's questions.

"What do you think of the proposed rearming?"

"Well," answered Lassen, choosing his words carefully, "I'm willing to listen to what Chairman Kruge has to say about it. If he's right about a possible invasion, we have a good reason to strengthen our defenses—we don't want to be subjugated again."

"But . . ." prodded Keneche.

"But," Lassen admitted, "I wonder if our troubled planet can bear the cost. I need to know more before my nation will support it—especially since Redland would be fueling the campaign with our energy resources."

"Well said, Delegate Lassen," Keneche affirmed. "I suggest that you consider all these things carefully."

Keneche took a moment to review his surroundings. The hallway was still full of delegates and their attendants discussing the day's meeting, but no one was close or seemed to be listening. Confident that their conversation was still secure, Keneche turned back to Lassen.

"Have you given much thought to candidates for the Minister of Energy Resources?" asked Keneche.

"That issue has not come up."

"But it is a responsible and important position that has been vacant since the inception of the charter seven years ago."

"Yes, I know, but there have been many other issues—" Lassen began to explain, and then cut himself off, deciding not to defend the Council on that point. He, too, was annoyed that no action had been taken to find a government leader to administer the energy resources. His nation possessed 80 percent of the energy on the planet—and about 90 percent of the Redlyn. The Redlyn deposits were among the richest in the civilized galaxy. They had been exploited by the Dominion, but were still vast. Now that Vassir was free of the Dominion, the Redlanders wanted to make sure the deposits would be used profitably and would not be a tempting target for another invader.

"I hope you'll be happy with the choice when it's made," said Keneche, something in his voice still betraying hidden meanings.

"Of course I'll be satisfied—I'll be involved in selecting him," said Lassen, frowning.

"Are you sure you'll be involved in the selection?" Keneche pumped.

"Of course, the charter—"

"Have you read the charter carefully concerning this matter?"

"Well, I think so," returned Lassen, nearly stammering.

"I've spent days studying the charter lately," said Keneche, choosing his words so that they would say just enough and no more. "It's a fascinating document. I urge you to read it again. You don't have to read it all, only the parts that interest, or should I say, concern you." Before Lassen had a chance to reply, he saw that Keneche had spotted a young man nearby dressed in the government center uniform. A small tatoo on the young man's forehead revealed that he was one of Chairman Kruge's slaves—probably bought from the Pirate Cartell and then branded with Kruge's name.

"Very good, sir," said Keneche to Lassen, straightening up and raising his voice. "I will inform your household of your imminent arrival. Are there any provisions you would have me prepare for your return trip to Redland?"

Lassen, bewildered by Keneche's abrupt change of topics, simply shook his head. He watched Keneche bow and exit the hallway swiftly, but the boy's haunting warning lingered in Lassen's mind.

Chapter Two

Promise me you won't go or I'll give these bandages a good yank," Lista threatened sternly. She had her arms around Lam, wrapping strips of elastic cloth around his chest. After his beating the night before, Lista managed to get Lam to his room at the port town's less expensive inn. She was nearly hoarse from talking, trying to keep him awake because of his concussion.

"I probably don't even have a broken rib," mumbled Lam.

"Not yet, maybe," Lista said sternly. "But I'm tempted to give you one. You should be resting—certainly not running to the port after your pistol."

Lam was about to complain about being told what to do, but didn't have the chance. "If those thugs find out you're armed, they won't just kick you a couple of times, they'll shoot you!" Lista tugged on the bandages a little tighter than she needed to, and Lam inhaled sharply.

"Remember, you're the newcomer around here."

Lam grunted. "If I felt any more welcome, I'd have broken legs, too."

"I don't know who those thugs were, but they're from the nation of Highland, just north of my home nation of Woodland on Vassir."

"I suppose you could tell by the way they punched."

"No, from their accents. But believe me, there's reason not to upset anyone from Highland right now."

"What's happening that you haven't told me about?" Lam asked.

"Maybe I'll tell you if you promise to stay," she replied, feeling the bandage to make sure it was secure.

"Maybe later. Thanks for the bandage," said Lam, rising to

his feet. As he stood, everything in the room seemed to lurch. Lam grasped Lista's shoulders to keep from falling while he waited for the room to hold still. When he felt he could stand on his own, he let go and looked away from her. Lista sighed in resignation. She knew that even if he had to lean against walls the whole way, he was going to Starjumper for his pistol.

Lam pulled his tunic off the back of the chair and strained it stiffly over his head.

"I'll meet you at the camp," Lam said curtly.

"I hope so," Lista whispered. "I'll make sure Me'Ben is there."

"Good." He walked to the door and pulled it open, shading his eyes against the Neecian sun now pouring into his room. He turned to Lista, and without looking at her said, "I'm sorry. I guess having my ribs kicked in puts me in a bad mood."

"It doesn't matter," she replied with the same lack of enthusiasm as Lam's apology had. He paused in the doorway for a moment, staring at the rough planks in the floor.

"Bye," he said finally as he turned to leave.

"Be careful," Lista urged. Lam nodded as he left, knowing that Lista would not be able to see his nonverbal promise.

When the door closed, Lista sighed and sat down on the edge of Lam's bed. Her fingers found the tiny locket that dangled from her neck and rubbed it nervously.

That man doesn't know what he's doing, she mused to herself. *You don't dance within a claw's swipe of a hungry Bashamta. That's what these people are—beasts who don't care whom they rip open.*

She lay back on the bed and thought how kind and reasonable Lam seemed to be when she first met him. The only thing that used to bother her about him was the way he refused to talk about himself, about his past. It didn't take much to convince him that the peaceful Be'Nay were not responsible for Altua's disappearance. In fact, he seemed concerned about them and wanted to know if Altua had told them about the Source and the Power.

Lista sighed again and wished that she could devote herself to a god. It just never seemed to do anyone any good. Of course, this Source seemed genuinely different than the conceited deities they worshiped on Vassir—Lam even called him "Friend."

"Some friend you are," Lista accused, her voice sounding hollow as it echoed off the blank walls of the empty room. "If you're there, I expect to see a little more out of you. Lam put his faith in you—and all it got him was being beaten up. What will happen if I believe in you? Things can't get much worse for me— I'm already a fugitive, blind orphan."

Lista waited for a reply, but none came.

"And while we're on the subject, where is Altua? He's supposedly one of your ambassadors. You're no more powerful than our old gods if you can't defend your own. Lam cared about you once, and I think he cared about me—now I don't know what he cares about." Lista sighed again.

"I'm tired of running—tired of being alone. I'm sick of being afraid. I thought things were getting better when I met Lam, but now look at what's happening. Friend, if *you* care about *him*, please protect him, even if he is stubborn."

Lista got up reluctantly. It certainly had not been a restful night, tending a battered—and bitter—man. She touched the circlet around her head to activate the finder, picked up her satchel, and stepped outside. The warmth on her skin told her that the sun was shining and she felt a warm breeze brush past her, bringing the scents from nearby flowers. It was the kind of day that would normally make her happy, but now she only hoped that she could find Me'Ben.

Lam made it to the spaceport lobby before he had to sit down. He had hoped that he could blend into the crowd, but he was only one of a few people using the small spaceport that day. A mother and her young son sat nearby. Lam guessed that the boy was born on Neece and his mother was taking him to Vassir to meet relatives or go to school. The port lobby, made mostly of wood planks from Neecian trees, provided a rustic contrast to the few pieces of advanced equipment necessary for running a spaceport.

One of the devices was a large, flat screen in the corner near the ceiling that flashed information about the arriving and departing ships. Lam rested his head on the back of the bench he was sitting on and watched the letters scamper across the screen.

Although they were in Common, he paid no attention to what they said; his only goal was to reach his own ship and retrieve his Redlyn pistol. He had not used it since he and his friends from Tsu fought the Dominion—he wanted to leave it in storage after that terrible victory. Now something in him wanted to get it back—and maybe use it on a certain three men if they gave him reason to.

As he stared at the screen, his mind wandering, the letters stopped and the picture changed to a symbol that Lam did not recognize—a six-pointed star on a field of dark red, with graceful runes inscribed at each point. Superimposed over the hexagram were two spheres, one in front of the other and casting a shadow on it. A voice crackled from a voicecaster near the screen.

"Please stand by for a personal message from Chairman Kruge of the Council of Delegates."

The woman with the child looked a little panicked and stiffened in attention.

Looking around the room, Lam saw that there were a couple of others who did not show the same respect. One man, who was sweeping the wood floors, spat in the corner and muttered, "Whose planet is this anyway?" The man behind the counter who seemed to be coordinating schedules did not even look up from his work to watch the most powerful government leader of their sister planet.

"Fellow Vassirians, friends," began a low, strong voice from the viewing screen in the corner. *This must be Kruge*, thought Lam. The screen showed the top half of a tall, thin man at the upper end of middle age. His eyes were the same steely gray as his hair. A huge banner with the hexagram and globes served as a dramatic backdrop for Kruge as he grasped the sides of the podium and addressed his audience. When he spoke, he over-emphasized each consonant to make sure there was no way his words would be misunderstood. Lam thought the authority in Kruge's voice bordered on arrogance.

"Our solar system is glorious. It is among the richest in resources; its people are strong and noble, and the gods have chosen us to be leaders in the galaxy. But I don't have to tell you that we face many ills. We have only recently been released from the stranglehold of the Dominion. They raped our fair planets—exploiting their resources and brutalizing our people."

The scene on the screen changed to a pan of Kruge's audience. It was a huge crowd assembled in a plaza and spilling into the streets. The voices of thousands muttered angrily in assent.

"Many of you listening to me this day have nowhere to sleep, little to eat, and little hope for the future. To make matters worse, the military has reported to me some distressing news relating to our security. From the base on Elna, that fair moon above Vassir, and also from our agents on Vassir and Neece, I have received reports that a foreign power is even now preparing to take over our solar system. Our resources make a tempting target. But we alone will choose the destiny of our planets. We are lords of our lands!"

Lam was enraptured by the intensity growing in Chairman Kruge's face and words. Kruge's skin was flushed and the muscles in his neck tensed as he continued.

"I believe our destiny is for greatness, for wealth, and for security once more. Some of you may doubt what I say, but I challenge you to believe it. Dare to believe it! Maybe you have no bed to lie on tonight, but not for long. Not if we have the courage to follow our destiny, to be masters of our planets." Kruge's voice became distorted by the voicecaster as it raised the volume so he could be heard over the frenzied crowd.

"I have been in discussion with the Council of Delegates, and we will soon make sweeping reforms on our planets. This is not just a new set of laws or a few wishful plans. This is a new way to live! A way to be conquerors instead of conquered! Victors instead of victims!

"These reforms are in the areas of global security, resource management, economic reform, and leadership in government. We plan to build a massive defense system to be based in orbit and on the ground. We will enlarge and equip the armies of Vassir and make our planets invulnerable! The second area is resource management. We will develop the energy, food, and human resources of our planets until there is more than enough for us, so that we can reestablish a lucrative trade with friendly powers in the civilized galaxy. We will save our resources for those *deserving* of them, those who will be able to contribute to the glory of our solar system, or those who have contributed so much already that they deserve their reward."

As Lam listened to the stirring words, he imagined the desperate people of Vassir absorbing Kruge's speech, clinging to it for hope. Kruge had the opposite affect on Lam. Something in his manner, his philosophy reminded him too much of his old enemy Kurdon. The men were worlds apart and did not even look alike, but Kruge seemed a natural enemy of the Way of Tsu, just as Kurdon had. For a moment, Lam reflected on the Way of Tsu—he knew he should ask the Friend what to do about Kruge, the men who beat him, what to do about Lista, and of course, Altua. But he brushed the thought aside and turned his attention back to Kruge.

"As for economic reform," continued Kruge, "we plan to put every capable person to work. Everyone will receive a livable wage, and a new currency will make a wage worth receiving. Finally, we plan on providing the strong and daring leadership needed to make us the masters. The weak and uncommitted of our solar systems will be given a choice: they can participate in the improvement and defense of our planets, or they will have to make room for the selfless and the courageous who will once again make our planets great!"

Lam knew exactly what "weak and uncommitted" people Kruge spoke of. The Vassirians blamed the natives on Neece for their defeat when the Dominion attacked. The Be'Nay people of Neece were very slow to commit themselves to anything, as Lam found out earlier when speaking with them about the Source, the Power, and the Friend. They also strove to avoid conflict at all costs, so they did not join the Vassirians in their resistance to the Dominion.

It's not fair to blame the Be'Nay, thought Lam. *It took the Power to destroy the Dominion—they wouldn't have stood a chance even if the Be'Nay had joined the fight. The Vassirians just need someone to blame.*

Kruge continued, but his speech was just passionate rhetoric that knotted Lam's stomach so he quietly rose from his bench and walked back to the counter where the Vassirian settler was absorbed in his screen. He was a sour-looking man with heavy glasses—there was nothing so advanced as vision correctors on Neece.

"I own Starjumper, and I would just like to check it over," Lam told the attendant at the counter. The man barely looked over his lenses at Lam, instead, just slid a plate of glass across the counter. The plate was attached by a cable to the attendant's screen which beeped twice when Lam placed his palm against it.

"Go ahead," the attendant authorized curtly. As Lam walked past the desk to the doors leading to the port's pad, he saw that the attendant was studying him suspiciously.

Perhaps it is just that they have few visitors who are not Vassirian, Lam tired to convince himself, but inside he knew there was more to it. He wished he could tell who was from Highland the way Lista could. The whole settlement probably knew about his beating, and Lam wondered how many knew of other assaults planned for him if he didn't stop "asking questions." He pushed through the doors and stepped out onto the space-pad pavement. Starjumper was easy to spot; it was one of the only ships there. Its white hull gleamed in the sun, and Lam's spirits rose as he hurried to join it.

From the air, it looked as if the ground had cracked and bubbles of molten metal and glass had been squeezed out and then solidified. As Lassen's shuttle neared Crystalia's private port, the outlines of the buildings became clearer. The domes and spires rose from the richest Redlyn mine on Vassir.

Long ago the mine had been carved into the hills. The meadows, marshes and woods came to an abrupt halt when they reached the mine where the ground had been peeled back to reveal the rich Redlyn deposits beneath. Now the Redlanders worked the mine underground, and buildings that supported the mining operation stood on the naked land. Domes made of clay, stone, and glass—used for living, refining, and processing—clustered together, punctuated in places with spires that rose gracefully into the sky.

Transports bore loads of earth containing the precious crystals from the cavernous mouth of the mine to the various processing plants. Other vehicles transported weary, grimy miners home to their families. In the distance, craters, now mostly filled with water, blemished the countryside.

Crystalia's beauty was stark. Any attempts at adorning the city had been abandoned under the Dominion. Then the city simply struggled to produce Redlyn to power the Dominion's war machine. Now it struggled to survive.

But the will to survive could be seen in the soiled faces of the miners as they walked doggedly from the mine's mouth to their waiting transports. In one way it was Lassen's mine—he had inherited it from his father who was killed by the Doomen in the battle for the mine over 15 years ago. In a deeper way, it was Redland's mine—it and every mine like it in the nation. Redland was proud.

Lassen's shuttle settled gracefully on the pad, and Lassen and his companion were soon stepping to the ground of their home.

A breeze off Unity Bay in Northern Redland tempered the afternoon heat that day. Lassen liked to take advantage of the pleasant weather—the next day the wind could be from the west off the desert.

"Let's walk to the compound instead of taking a transport," suggested Lassen to Jihrmar, his cousin and counselor, an almost black-complexioned man about Lassen's age with lively brown eyes. "It will give us a chance to review the operation—we have to make sure it has not gone too well while we were away."

Jihrmar laughed. "That's right. If things go too well, people will wonder what we're paid for."

Lassen told the rest of their traveling party to meet them back at the compound, and then struck off down the street.

"Things are slowly returning to normal," said Jihrmar, taking in the entire mining town with his gesture.

"It has been slow," Lassen agreed. "But it's improving. The Dominion was thorough. It's a wonder they didn't manage to leech all the Redlyn from the planet."

"It's not as if they didn't try," Jihrmar said, his eyes revealing some of his private rage. "Working our people until they died of exhaustion, blasting craters in the countryside looking for new deposits."

"But we survived," said Lassen, pride now lightening the conversation. Signs of Redland's pride were displayed everywhere. Banners with the Redland seal, a Redlyn crystal with a tree growing from it, hung from nearly every building. Absent was the Vassirian flag—the hexagram with the two worlds superimposed over it. The streets and buildings were stained from the mining activities, and a few buildings still had wounds from the brief battle with Doomen soldiers the miners fought there years before. But the inhabitants of the mining town kept things as clean as possible, and some of the buildings had small flower gardens in front of them.

"I almost hate to bring it up again," started Lassen as he and Jihrmar continued walking down the narrow street toward the compound where he and his family lived. Lassen waited for a noisy transport to lumber past above their heads before he continued. "We've been talking too much about Vassir's trouble. For days that's all we've been doing with the mine owners and rulers in Redland to find out what they think should be done. After Kruge's speech last night, it seems like it was all a waste of time."

"The Master Planet Speech," Lassen's aide interjected, using the nickname it had already picked up.

"Yes. And the more I think about it, the angrier I become. The Council of Delegates had not decided on anything final about the plans for the currency or for rearming, and he broadcasts it to the world. To two worlds! Where does that leave the Council in the decision-making?"

"I'd be at least as angry as you are," Jihrmar assured him, nodding his short black curls. "And I understand that you're not the only one Kruge upset. Only two days ago, Cruzan the Valorian Master publicly denounced Chairman Kruge's plans as being hasty and unwise. I've heard rumors that right after his statement, he disappeared along with some of his closest family and followers. Cruzan isn't just a Highland military leader—he's a spiritual leader, one of the most cohesive forces on Vassir. Of course, the rumor might not be true. But if it is true, there's more trouble than we even imagine."

Lassen stopped suddenly as a brightly colored ball rolled

across their path. Several children chased the ball closely, laughing and yelling at each other as they competed for the colorful prize. One of them stopped and stared at Lassen, apparently recognizing him as Crystalia's master.

"You'd better hurry," said Lassen, squatting to speak with the child face-to-face. "They have a good head start on you— you may not catch up for days!" The serious-faced youngster gazed at the delegate for another moment and then raced after his comrades. Lassen chuckled as he stood. They struck off again and Jihrmar continued.

"You and I have had many discussions about Redland and Vassir. We had decided that things were finally improving. The mines are producing well and the citizens seem to have gotten over the Dominion—their confidence is returning and they are beginning to invest themselves in their land again."

"And now Chairman Kruge is spreading this paranoia about foreign invasion," added Lassen in disgust. "He hasn't shared with *us* his secret sources who say we will be invaded, but he expects us to devote our resources to rearming. Instead, we should be trading with other planets and systems, building our economy, not spending on ourselves."

Jihrmar nodded his understanding. "Anyway," Lassen continued, "you'd better hope it's not true—you are commander of the militia if it comes to a fight."

"We're ready," Jihrmar announced confidently. They walked quietly together for a while. Once in a while the sun spilled through the spaces between the buildings as if it were trying to wash the street to give them a more pleasant homecoming. Jihrmar shaded his eyes with his dark-skinned arm and splashed golden reflections from his bracelet on the stone walls around them. A sunburst carving in the bracelet identified him with his mother's homeland of Sundor, one of Redland's southern neighbors. Although he was only half Redlander, Jihrmar was wholly committed to it.

"What about the Minister of Energy vacancy?" asked Jihrmar.

"I think such a person could be helpful if his or her motives were just," replied Lassen. "But after the last Council meeting,

I read over the charter—especially concerning the nominating and election of this position. As incredible as it sounds, we have no real say in the nomination and no veto power on the choice!"

"Do you think that's by design?" Jihrmar asked quietly as they neared Lassen's compound. Lassen paused by the intricately wrought metal gate that spanned a gap in the stone wall which surrounded the compound.

"I'm not sure I care. I hate to start a controversy. For one thing, we have more than enough to do here in Crystalia without inventing problems. For another, Chairman Kruge is the one with the most responsibility in the governing of this planet—I feel we should be supporting him, not questioning his motives. But I *am* rather unsettled by the way things are going. I'm beginning to get the feeling that something is very wrong."

Before Lassen had a chance to swing the gate open himself, a bright-eyed, tousle-haired boy ran to the gate from inside the compound and heaved it open.

"Papa!" he squealed. Lassen glanced over to Jihrmar and shrugged his shoulders to say that their serious conversation was over. He bent down, swept the boy off the ground and held the giggling youngster upside down as he walked to his house. Lassen's wife waited at the door, smiling. She waved to Jihrmar and then followed her husband in.

Jihrmar stayed by the gate and watched his cousin—his friend—disappear through the doorway of his simple dwelling.

"I don't think it will be much longer before we don't have to invent controversies," he said quietly. "Plenty of them will slap us in the face soon enough."

Chapter Three

Lam paused in Starjumper's hatch. For a moment, he was assaulted with memories of his days as a pirate, of long hours in space, of riding with King Padeus and Max, of victorious space fights against Doomen ships.

"This always happens," he sighed as he headed to the rear of the ship. He pressed open the compartment that held extra clothes and pulled out his flight tunic. Usually he wore it, but lately he had given it up in favor of the rugged canvas jacket and trousers many of the Neecian settlers from Vassir wore. He fished in the pocket, retrieved a handful of items and went to sit down in the pilot's seat. He spread his treasures out on the control panel, leaned back and gazed at them. One was the amulet King Padeus had given him. The M-stone in it glowed only faintly. *I'm sure Altua has, or had, an M-stone that would make this one glow brighter if he were near*, Lam thought. Before his beating, Lam had asked dozens of settlers on Neece about the aged ambassador, and still the best information he had was from Lista who remembered he was leaving for somewhere. Lam had concluded that Altua had probably traveled to Vassir, but Vassir was a large planet, and he would need to know where to start looking if he went there. *I'll ask spaceport personnel, inn servants—anyone I can find*, he thought. *If anyone gives me trouble again, I'll be ready.*

Next to the M-stone amulet lay a smooth, flat stone with a three-cornered leaf etched into it. The Le-in had given it to him on the planet Refuge. They said it stood for the Source, the Power, and the Friend. The Friend! Lam had not thought much about him these last couple of days. He was angry over his beating and his failure to find Altua, and he felt guilty for his anger. Deep down he knew he should surrender his anger, but Lam put off the fleeting thoughts that urged him to turn his problems over to the Friend. Instead, he turned to the final trinket on the console. It was a delicate gold ring.

Lam picked up the ring and thought about the girl from his home planet who had given it to him. It was the only surviving remembrance of Entar—destroyed by the Dominion years ago. He recalled holding that ring and gazing out the portals into the vastness of space, thinking. Those pensive times brought a quiet, lonely feeling that he had learned to enjoy, even to depend upon.

Then he thought about the other woman who had suddenly entered his life. *Lista. Why did she have to confuse things?* He had not come to Neece to get involved with a woman.

"I didn't come to get beaten up, either," Lam muttered angrily. He clenched the ring in his fist, reached beneath his seat and pulled out his Redlyn pistol. It was Pirate Cartel-made—small, and so thin that it could be easily concealed. Lam did not stop to admire it, but shoved it into the back of his belt beneath his canvas jacket. He tucked the ring into his del pocket and left the ship, refusing to look back at the amulet and the etched stone that lay on the control panel.

Lam slipped out of the port without incident and struck off down the dirt path that led back to the town. Although it would be dangerous, he intended to report his beating to the Peace Enforcer. The sun was not high, but the day was at its warmest, rewarding his exertion with beads of sweat on his forehead and back.

Lam soon reached the town and turned onto the wood sidewalk that passed in front of all the buildings along the main street. The tavern was quiet this time of the afternoon, and he passed by. Lam glanced inside the hunting shop as he walked on and saw two men admiring a rifle that fired projectiles—used mostly for hunting medium-sized game. When the men noticed Lam, they quickly turned their heads the other way. Lam wished he knew if they were from Highland and why they looked away. For that matter, he wished he knew why any of this was happening to him.

Lam knew he had reached the Peace Enforcer's office by the

boots propped up on the windowsill. An awning attached to the clay façade stretched over the sidewalk and sheltered the dozing Enforcer from the hot afternoon sun. Lam looked at this man who was supposed to be a symbol of security in the settlement and didn't wonder that he had been beaten. Leather straps barely restrained the Enforcer's belly, and a large, military-style Redlyn pistol dangled from a strained belt.

Lam cleared his throat to get the Enforcer's attention. For a moment there was no response; then one eye opened to assess this intrusion on his relaxation.

"Well!" exclaimed the Peace Enforcer, his gravelly voice registering delight. "I expected to see you here." The balding officer pushed himself upright in his chair with some effort, but left his feet on his windowsill. He looked Lam in the eye. "I heard you had an incident the other night."

"Where did you hear that?" asked Lam suspiciously.

The Enforcer shrugged his shoulders. "This is a small community—word travels through it like lightning through a lake. Who can say who started it?"

Lam stood and waited for the reclining man to inquire further, but when he did not, Lam filled in the details.

"Lista NaWoodlander, the Restorer, and I were on the gravel road walking toward the town when we were jumped by three masked men, beaten up, and warned to stop asking questions about Altua." At this point Lam lifted his tunic just enough to show the bandages without revealing the pistol he had concealed near his back.

"I'll see what I can do about it," the Enforcer said, nearly yawning. He slouched in his chair again and closed his eyes. After a moment he opened the right one and eyed the stranger. "And if you want to find your ambassador, I'd suggest asking those native friends of yours."

"Thanks," Lam muttered, not at all grateful—or comforted.

"Lam Laeo, where are you?" demanded Lista of the air. She was back at the restoration camp outside of New Highland where she did what she could to help the ill of the Be'Nay. Even without the aid of her finder, she could tell it was getting to be night. The air that brushed against her face was cool, and the night insects were slowly beginning their nightly chorus.

Suddenly a twig snapped behind her. Lista drew a startled breath and turned in the direction of the footstep.

"Lam? Lam is that you?"

"That depends on if that's you, Lista," came the weary reply.

"I've been so worried!" she said as she ran to meet him. Lam's voice sounded much better than she thought it would.

"Watch the purple ribs," Lam laughed as he returned her embrace. He decided Lista wasn't as tough as she pretended.

"What took you so long?" asked Lista, pushing Lam away from her.

"I had an interesting encounter with the Peace Enforcer," Lam began. "But I also wanted to tell you that I saw a speech by our friend Chairman Kruge."

"What is he up to now?" sighed Lista in exasperation.

"Well, he's got some grand scheme to solve all the problems in the solar system. The only trouble is, there is not much room for the Be'Nay. And I felt more than a little uncomfortable with what he said about people having to be 'capable.' "

Lista turned away from Lam and walked to a log seat in the lean-to. She sat with her back toward Lam.

"What is it that you haven't told me?" Lam asked a little impatiently. He received silence and Lista's back.

"I'm sorry," he said. "I have no right to be angry with you. This is your planet—these are your troubles."

Lam sat next to her and put his arm around her shoulder. "But I would like to know what's been troubling you. Has it got to do with people who are not completely 'capable'?"

When he still received no reply, he withdrew his arm and sighed. Lista took his hand and pulled his arm around her again.

"Crips. On Vassir they call us Crips—everyone who's not completely 'normal.' " That was all Lista offered.

"Where's Me'Ben?" Lam asked, tired of trying to pry information out of the woman.

"He had some work to do for the Revered Ones before he came, but he promised to be here."

"Just as well," said Lam, rising from the log and sitting

down on a rough-hewn chair in the shelter of the lean-to. "I have more to tell you."

"Oh?"

"I had an enlightening encounter with the local public servant."

Lista listened as Lam told about getting his pistol from Starjumper and then dealing with the Peace Enforcer.

"So he didn't care that we were battered in his street?" asked Lista without much surprise when Lam was through with that part of his story.

"I was tempted to compare my bruises to the tread on his boots."

Lista sighed, rose from her seat and moved behind Lam, still seated in his chair. Bending over, she put her arms around him from behind, and he reached up and patted her hand.

"This is only the beginning of our trouble," Lista said wearily.

"Mesha? Sarin?" the two heard a voice call from the edge of camp, using the Be'Nay terms of respect for single men and women.

"Here, Me'Ben," Lista called back.

Moments later the powerful figure of the Neecian native stood before them, his dark eyes flashing. His muscles were barely covered by his leather vest, and his leather shorts were sewn with brightly colored quills as was the sheath for his knife strapped to his right thigh. Two rings pierced his right ear and identified him as a high-ranking assistant to the Revered Ones.

"Thank you for coming," said Lam as Me'Ben bowed slightly. Lam motioned for Me'Ben and his friend to sit down on a log across the fire pit from him.

"Are you aware of what happened to Lista and me?"

"Yes," answered Me'Ben. "The sorrow and well wishes of the Be'Nay we extend to you."

"Thank you," said Lam quickly. "But I am concerned for your people." Lam leaned forward in his chair and related his news intensely. "I saw Chairman Kruge of Vassir speaking on the viewing screen in the port. The Vassirian people blame the Be'Nay for losing the war against the Dominion. They're angry and afraid of being taken over again—I think you should make plans to defend yourselves."

"Of this blame we are aware, Sarin," responded the Be'Nay evenly, his rugged features betraying no emotion.

"Me'Ben," began Lam more urgently, "you are in danger!"

"We have outlived many dictators—including the Dominion. It is the position of the Revered Ones that we shall outlive the present danger as well and that we need not panic or take up arms."

Lam groaned in exasperation, leaned back in his chair and rubbed his face.

"While it is true that we do not question the Revered Ones," Me'Ben continued, "there may be differing interpretations of their position."

Lam looked up at Me'Ben. He could not read the Be'Nay very well, but it seemed to Lam that by the look on his face, Me'Ben had said much more than those few words.

"There is one other thing," added Me'Ben, looking Lam in the eyes and speaking very clearly. "The Revered Ones have also asked for a gathering with you concerning the Way of Tsu."

Lam's eyebrows raised in surprise; then he broke into a smile. "That's wonderful!" Lam exclaimed with unveiled delight.

The usually reserved Me'Ben laughed gently and said, "Mesha, I wish you could see our friend Lam; he has fallen out of his chair."

"I have not!" Lam defended himself and they all laughed together for a welcome moment.

"I can't pass up an opportunity to talk to your Revered Ones, Me'Ben," Lam said, still smiling from the Neecian's prank. "But my primary objective is still to find Altua, and I only have a few more people to talk to around here that might have some information."

"And if you ask the wrong question of the wrong person, Tsu might have to send someone here to find *you*," Lista warned.

Lam sat silently mulling over Lista's warning. He slipped his hand into the pocket of his canvas tunic and fingered the familiar lines of the pistol. The weapon didn't comfort him as much as he hoped it would.

Chapter Four

Lassen nodded to the guard at the Highland spaceport gate. The guard nodded back and quickly moved to shut down the energy barrier that surrounded the port. Lassen decided to walk the few blocks to the government center to give him extra time to think before he confronted Chairman Kruge.

Lassen thought about the com-link discussion he had had the day before with the delegate from Seaward. She had called him in a rage with news she was sure would be upsetting. It had been.

"I just found out that Chairman Kruge plans on nominating his son, Kaman, as Minister of Energy Resources," she had said, sounding as if she could hardly believe it herself.

"What? What is your source?" Lassen had demanded in dismay.

"I'm not sure I should say at this point," the Seawarder replied cautiously, "but it is a reliable one."

Just thinking about it again made Lassen flush in spite of the cloudy, cold Highland weather. How dare Kruge plan to nominate someone without consulting the Council—especially the delegate from Redland, the nation with the most at stake! And how could he dare nominate someone with no experience managing energy resources? It was becoming frighteningly evident to Lassen that Chairman Kruge had ambitions beyond merely presiding over the Council of Delegates. And it was becoming painfully clear that Lassen could no longer obediently endorse the Chairman's policies and quietly live his life.

The closer he got to the government center, the more people there were on the street. Public communal houses faced the street, and the destitute of Highland sat on their steps or stood idly by streetlights and listlessly watched him pass. Lassen became uneasy, although he tried not to show it, and he walked only a little faster. He puffed from the exertion, and steam from his breath trailed behind him. He tried not to think about how out of place he must look, and how wealthy compared to these who watched him. Lassen wore a lightweight, brightly colored tropical costume, jeweled belt and red delegate sash. The poor of Highland surrounding him wore used and dingy clothes, layered against the region's cold.

Just one more corner and one more block, thought Lassen. But when he reached the corner, he found himself near the end of a food line that stretched nearly a block. Old men leaned on sticks, proud young men patted their children's hair and, along with the youngsters, stared at the stranger.

At the head of the line stood two uniformed Highland militiamen, their shoulder blasters readied in front of them. They wore black, fur-lined caps and stood vigilant, moving only enough to keep their blood circulating. Lassen knew why they were there—Kruge had put strict controls on meetings and crowds in Highland. Only those that were necessary or specially licensed were allowed, and even those had to have guards. He had heard that even religious gatherings were limited and strictly controlled. Lassen was happy there were no such controls in Redland. No one showed much interest in religious gatherings anyway—the gods did not seem much interested in them. If they had been, they wouldn't have allowed the Dominion to ruin their planet.

"Excuse me," said Lassen. He stood and waited for the boys that blocked his path to stand aside and let him pass. The oldest of several folded his arms and curled his lip in a sneer. He did not move for Lassen. The other boys in that part of the food line stared at him with faces that masked their feelings. Lassen acted calm, but in his mind he planned what to do if he were jumped.

After a few long, tense moments, the older boy bowed with mock respect and motioned him through. The other boys did the same, and he passed through them while they snickered behind his back. Sheer force of will kept him from looking back to see if there were knives drawn on him.

"Hey, Redlander!" He heard someone call out from behind him. "Won't you stay for supper?" The belligerent invitation was followed by bitter laughter.

"Go easy on him," another shouted; "he's a long way from home—he might have had only four or five meals today!"

"Redlander! I hope a mine collapses on you!"

He steeled himself and pushed forward at a brisk pace. Soon all he heard was the cruel laughter.

"The delegate from Redland is here to see you," announced Keneche over the com-link. Kruge's son was alert to his father's reaction. He knew that his half-brother Kaman was in his study with him, and he hoped to learn something of their plans.

"Tell him I will be with him shortly," the Chairman responded. Before the connection broke, Keneche heard the two laughing, as if Lassen's visit were a source of some amusement.

"He will be with you—" began Keneche.

"Shortly. Yes, I heard." Lassen stood in front of the arc-shaped desk where Keneche was seated, voluntarily filling in for his half sister who was usually stationed there. Keneche knew this was an important day to keep an eye on his father. He motioned an invitation for Lassen to sit on a padded, fur-covered bench in the room and offered him some ice water.

"Thank you."

Keneche placed a glass under a stone fountain set into the wall, and the spouting water filled the vessel.

"I know why you are here," whispered Keneche, barely audible over the splashing water. "I also know what will happen." Keneche handed him his glass, and simultaneously handed him a slip of parchment with a com-link reference number on it. Lassen glanced at the note and slipped it into his tunic pocket.

"You seem to know many things, Krugeson," Lassen noted dryly. "And you seem to be drawn to trouble like a Night Snapper to honey."

"Call it a family trait," Keneche said with a grin.

"Speaking of your family, ever since you mentioned her, I've been wondering about your mother. I understand one of

Chairman Kruge's wives is the daughter of Cruzan, the Valorian Master, and that they're both missing."

"Just forget about the Valorians!" Keneche snapped. "And let's leave my mother out of this."

At that moment, Chairman Kruge's door swung open and the Chairman's tall, gaunt form filled the doorway.

"Welcome, Lassen!" he said almost sincerely.

"Thank you," he responded. Rising to his feet he handed his still-full glass to Keneche. Kruge grasped Lassen's forearm in greeting as Lassen did the same and followed him into the Chairman's study.

"Sit, sit," Kruge insisted. Lassen obeyed and looked around the room. Kaman apparently had ducked out a different exit.

Kruge's study made only a weak show of order. His papers and reference materials were piled on shelves that lined the wall. The closed window curtains added gloom to the disarray.

The Chairman lowered himself into his seat behind a table topped with gray stone. A large red banner displaying the black hexagram and globes hung behind him on the wall. Several monitor screens around the room were dark, their purpose veiled.

"Tell me what brings you here," probed Kruge, leaning back in his reclining seat. Although polite, Kruge was in no mood for pleasantries.

"Well, Chairman—" began Lassen hesitantly. After all his thought, he still was not able to bring up the subject delicately. He plunged. "It is my understanding that you have selected a candidate for Minister of Energy Resources."

Kruge folded his hands and tapped his forefingers against his lips.

"It is very interesting that you should have heard that. I actually have not made any decisions, but yes, I do have a candidate in mind. If you have heard that much, you probably also know that I am considering nominating Kaman."

"Yes, that is what I have heard. And I think it would be unwise for you simply to nominate your son without at least examining other candidates."

"I will ignore your insult concerning my wisdom for the moment," said Kruge stiffly, "and tell you that there really is no reason to consider other candidates."

"What about appearance?" asked Lassen, leaning forward in his seat. "What about fairness?"

"The charter is quite clear on this process," responded Kruge, raising his voice and swinging his seat around to face Lassen more directly. "I bring the nomination to the Council of Delegates and they say yes or no. It is that simple. Their decision, I think, will be simple as well."

"There must be other candidates worth considering," pleaded Lassen. "What about someone from the mining industry? I know two who have been involved in governing—"

Kruge interrupted Lassen and leaned forward over his stone-topped table. "It would not be fair to the other candidates to pretend to consider them. And there is no reason to consider them—Kaman is far superior. We work well together; he knows this government, and the people know him."

"People will take it wrong if Kaman is appointed to this position." The futility Lassen felt crept into his voice.

"There is no room for such people in the New Vassir!" growled Kruge, and a menacing coldness sprang into his steely eyes. Then the Chairman leaned back in his chair, and the sharpness vanished as quickly as it had appeared. "Is there anything else?"

This was a side of Chairman Kruge Lassen had not seen before, and it shook him. He breathed deeply, trying to calm himself.

"I think I should tell you that the nation of Redland has concerns over the use of our resources for rearming."

Kruge stared past Lassen to the Vassirian banner on the wall. He barely nodded to acknowledge Lassen's words as the Redland delegate relayed the concerns of his nation.

"We believe that our economy would improve even more rapidly if we traded our energy resources with other systems instead of using them here on Vassir."

When Lassen was through, Kruge repeated simply, "Is there anything else?"

"No," Lassen replied, his voice weak from passion, his face livid. "There doesn't seem to be."

"Keneche will get you a transport to your shuttle."

Lassen thrust his hands into his tunic pockets as he stormed from Kruge's study. But his expression changed from rage to determination when he felt the parchment that Keneche had slipped him.

Chairman Kruge sat brooding behind his stone-topped table, watching the monitors on the wall of his study. On the screens, he saw Lassen storm down the hall and reach the main stairway that looked over the three-story entry plaza. The hexagram banners draped over the railings of each floor's balcony stirred lightly; drafts always plagued such an immense building. A light drizzle had begun to fall, forming cold droplets on the window beside the stairway.

Kruge expected anger from Lassen; in the end it would give him the excuse that he needed to get Lassen out of the way and put his son in charge of energy resources. The Redlanders were just too independent to manage. Fifteen years under one government—the Dominion—had not broken them of that. He would have to teach them, and all the little nations of Vassir and Neece, to appreciate his vision for unity in the solar system.

Kruge smiled when he thought about his Utopia—a united and powerful Vassir. How close they were to achieving it! But his smile faded when he turned his attention back to Lassen, now almost to the bottom of the stars. A door at the far end of Kruge's study creaked and Kaman stepped back into his father's presence and sat across from him.

"He's done as much for this planet as a stone in the road," Kruge muttered. "All he does is get in the way of progress. What right does he have to complain?"

Kruge settled back into his seat, and Kaman watched Lassen leave. "Maybe he will get sick from the cold and die," Kruge speculated. "Lassen is like the human refuse we used for research while I was governor under the Dominion. The weak and cowardly like him will make way for the new Vassir—just as the cripples, the idiots, and the insane will." Kaman nodded his agreement soberly.

When Kruge saw that Lassen was gone, he rubbed his eyes with his palms and then leaned forward to the com-link on the same black panel that controlled the monitors.

"Keneche, come in here. I have an errand for you immediately," Kruge spoke into the small cloth-covered pick-up. Silence answered.

"Keneche, are you out there?" Kruge switched a monitor to view the reception room. The desk was vacant. "It's just as well," he finally grumbled to Kaman; "he'd probably make a mess of it anyway."

The less-appealing and generally ignored accomplishments of Wyntir's architects snaked underneath its streets and buildings. Not even the city workers knew much about the sewers anymore. Keneche was an exception. His footsteps echoed down a damp stone tunnel that seemed to stretch into infinity. As he walked, small reptiles and large furry creatures scampered from the light he carried in one hand. In the other, he held a military-style Redlyn pistol for any pest that might not wish to yield its territory. The pistol was almost an antique, but it worked. He had secretly bought it from a colorful peddler who had visited Wyntir the year before, bartering kitchen utensils, jewelry, and contraband weapons. It cost him three new Redlyn rod packs for the trader's skip, but he was proud of his purchase.

Keneche pulled up the hood of his tunic, partly because of the chill and partly to stop the vile water from dripping on his head as he walked. *I'm glad I packed the food in a double wrap*, he thought to himself as the runoff from the city dripped onto the pack strapped to Keneche's back. He scanned the walls around him with his lamp and finally found what he was looking for— a set of metal rungs leading up.

The metal was slippery, and Keneche had to abandon his lamp so that he could use both hands. His boots chinked against the rungs as he ascended. Only a few steps up he could already feel the warmth. The downdraft brought with it smells of perfume and freshly cooked food.

A closed metal portal over his head kept Keneche from climbing any farther, and he tapped out a rhythmic message. It quickly opened and light spilled onto him as four hands reached down to lift him up.

"Good to see you, boy!" said one older male voice.

"Welcome, son," said a woman tenderly.

When his eyes had adjusted, he looked around. Ten or more people populated that room, and hallways led to other rooms. The room itself had once been a water and waste control station, but it had been converted—with the help of rugs, tapestries, and furniture—into a somewhat comfortable room. Portable lights and heaters made the squat stone cells livable.

"I brought more food and supplies," announced Keneche cheerfully as he dropped his pack onto a table and began to remove its valuable contents.

A distinguished-looking elderly man in casual Highland military clothes put his hand on Keneche's shoulder.

"You endanger yourself by coming here."

"Please, Grandfather," replied Keneche. "It's the least I could do after the way you've taken care of my mother and me." The woman, wearing colorful, fur-lined Highland clothes with a laced-up tunic, put her arm around Keneche and smiled.

"I feel so bad that you all have to hide here," Keneche continued. "It's like a prison. At least it is a more comfortable prison than my father gives his enemies—which is what you'd have if he knew you were still in the city. His grip is getting tighter by the day. He would not tolerate your opposition, even if you are Cruzan, the Valorian Master."

Keneche's mother motioned for him to join her in the corner of their small room.

"You know I don't like you so alone in that government center," she said to him earnestly and in low tones. "Your life is in danger every moment."

"Mother," Keneche scolded, "you know I have several contacts and confidants at the center. None of them know where you are, but they're sharing the risk with me. Some of those people are in pretty high places, too. Besides, it won't be long, and you and Grandfather will be able to come back—the people will be shouting for Cruzan, the mighty Valorian Master."

"Well, until that time comes, I want you to be very careful— I'm sure you are more my son than Kruge's son to them."

"I'll be careful, Mother," Keneche promised and pecked his

mother on the cheek. "I'll see you all again soon."

He walked back to the ladder, and as he passed one of the tiny, dimly lit rooms off the living area, he saw gleaming gold pieces of armor hanging from hooks. There was no other suit like it in Highland—or anywhere on Vassir, and even the glimpse he caught in passing thrilled him.

Someday, if we survive this ordeal, I'm going to be a Valorian, he promised himself.

Lassen studied Siah, the delegate from Seaward, as she sat opposite him in the solarium of his compound. Her short, black curls rose and fell like the waves of the ocean her nation bordered. Her dark green eyes revealed a similar tempest, a warning that she was ready for a fight. A long, airy coat of shiny pastels touched the burnt-red tile of the floor and nearly covered her loose-fitting pants of the same airy material. A bright rose cape with drawstring hood was clasped around her neck by a golden fish pin, and the cape itself was slung over her shoulders. The only jewelry she wore was a tiny white crystal set in silver and pierced into the right side of her slender nose.

"You're the only delegate I know I can speak with in confidence," said Lassen.

"I appreciate your confidence," she hastily replied. "But it will take more than you and me to stop the Chairman's headlong rush into power. We have to do something as a Council to force him to listen to our concerns."

"It may be difficult to get the others to do anything resembling opposition to Chairman Kruge. You know how he has done us all favors."

"He tried to buy us, you mean," admitted Siah. "He swayed the Council to liberate funds for repairing our northern dikes — the ones the Dominion destroyed. And he lent you Highland troops to clear the Gymstien mine. There are other delegates who owe him much deeper debts."

"But we wouldn't be asking them to help depose him—just to limit his authority somewhat and make him more responsive to the nations."

The Seaward delegate leaned forward and put her glass

down on the table between them.

"You sound like you have a scheme."

"Hardly a 'scheme.' I'd like to see a special league assigned to deal with specific social and economic problems—a totally nongovernmental group made up of representatives of each of our nations."

"How can that work?" she asked, leaning back in her chair in near resignation. "You know he schedules the delegate meetings and totally plans their agenda. Do you think he will place such a suggestion on the table?"

"No," admitted Lassen, "but perhaps we could get a statement requesting such an action signed by other delegates. This would give us time to discuss the matter with the others at length first—although I'll admit I deeply dread opposing Chairman Kruge to his face. You can bet I'll be expecting the worst from him."

The Seaward delegate folded her arms and lowered her head in concentration.

"It might work," she said softly without raising her head. Then she looked up and stated, "I'm not intimidated by Kruge, but who do you think we can persuade to sign such a document?"

A soft, blue glow illuminated the dreary cell. A long snake-like creature half crept, half slithered across the damp floor, its tongue probing the air. It encountered the heavy links of a metal chain and propped its top half on them, turning its pointed head one way and then the other. A groan from the other side of the room startled the beast and it leaped over the chain and escaped down a grilled hole in the corner.

The pathetic form attached to the chain slid up, leaning against the slimy stone wall, and groaned a second time. He sat in his own filth, and an unkempt beard lay matted against his chest.

"Is there someone there?" he stammered feebly. "I'm— thirsty; water, please?" No one answered. No one was there.

"How long are you going to keep me here? What can I do— what conditions must be met before I am released?"

He had been drifting in and out of a deprivation-induced sleep for days.

Gradually realizing that he had again hallucinated a human visitor, the man sighed shakily and attempted to calm himself— he needed to conserve all the energy he could.

"All beauty to the Source," the ancient-looking man croaked in something resembling a song. "And might to the Power." Gasping for breath after that incredible effort, he lapsed into merciful unconsciousness.

The dim, blue light came from an M-stone set in an amulet that hung about his neck. In Tsuian script beneath the stone was one word: Altua.

Chapter Five

Lassen stole nervous glances at Siah, the Seaward delegate, throughout the entire meeting. His heart was not in the business being discussed; he was thinking about the statement he and several other delegates had signed requesting a nongovernmental league to propose direction to the Council of Delegates. To his annoyance, gathering the few signatures had taken most of his time—time he felt should have been spent directing his mine. To make matters worse, Kruge had not even mentioned the document during the entire meeting.

He watched Chairman Kruge dispose of the business enthusiastically and efficiently. Kruge would propose a program or plan and be ready with pat answers to all the delegates' concerns. The streamlined process that Lassen had always appreciated before now made him sick.

He had sent the statement to Kruge by special courier several days before, and as the meeting inched closer to the appointed closing time, Lassen realized that Kruge's strategy toward the document was to ignore it. The meeting went so smoothly, and the delegates and Kruge were so congenial, Lassen almost wondered if the matter were important enough for him to bring up.

"Are there any other affairs before we close our session for the evening?" asked Kruge innocently. Lassen knew this was his only chance.

"I am told that you received a document yesterday that detailed some recent concerns some of us have been feeling," said Lassen as evenly as he could. Kruge looked in Lassen's direction, but stared past him to the wall. The Chairman remained silent and expressionless. The other delegates looked nervously at the two men and waited for someone to say something.

Finally Kruge forced a brief laugh and repeated his earlier question, "Is there any more business? It's almost time to adjourn for the evening."

"I believe the delegate from Redland raised some business, Chairman Kruge," asserted Siah firmly. Lassen looked at her with respect. He was on the verge of yelling, or leaving, or trembling, but Siah fixed a steady gaze into Kruge's dun eyes.

"Most of us are here because we care about Vassir, and we have dedicated ourselves to seeing that she becomes what she can be." Kruge's voice was raised, and the veins in his neck and temples protruded. "This refuse of a document to which you refer is a time-waster. It does not even deserve to be discussed."

"But there are legitimate concerns—" Lassen attempted to interject, but Kruge drowned him out.

"Those of you who have disgraced your name with this document are creating division—something deadly to us as we prepare for a new and secure Vassir," Kruge ranted. "Remember why you are delegates and the vows you took to serve Vassir!" He rose to his feet and declared, "It is now closing time, and this meeting is ended!"

Lassen opened his mouth to protest, but at Kruge's signal, two Highland soldiers entered the room with shoulder blasters readied in front of them.

"You will now be shown to your rooms," fumed the still-flushed Chairman.

Lassen rose silently, collected his notes and obediently followed his "escort." As he passed Kruge, he hoped to meet his eyes and wordlessly communicate his anger. Kruge did not look up from shuffling his own papers.

Lassen paced in his room—a nicely furnished room, reserved for honored visitors to the government center. But right now it was a jail cell. Lassen's face was expressionless as he paced, but burning eyes revealed his fury.

He strode to the door and listened. Somewhere far down the hall he heard shouts mingled with the high-pitched whines of Redlyn weapons discharging. Small explosions and the sound of more gunfire followed. Lassen smiled grimly—it was what he had been waiting for.

The sounds of the battle neared. The panicked shouts of the government center guards rose above the crashing and the screaming weapons. The smell of burning wood drifted beneath his door and Lassen knew the battle had reached him. He jumped back as shoulder blaster bolts smashed the door to slivers. A frightening figure in highly polished black armor stormed into the room through the fragmented door, his shoulder blaster pointed at Lassen's neck.

For a tense moment Lassen looked at his own eyes reflected in the intruder's lowered visor. The figure then handed Lassen his weapon and swung another down from his back, aimed at the window and fired several times. Shards of glass spilled into the courtyard below, along with much of the brick that framed the window. Lassen and his rescuer ran for the smoldering gash and looked out. Lights from a hovering shuttle flooded them as it swiftly drew closer, its side door wide open.

The powerful figure's arrival assured Lassen that his escape would be successful. His burnished black armor glared in the floodlights. The commando was a Valorian, well trained in physical might, courage, and the mysterious Valorian discipline. No weapon on Vassir could give a man confidence in combat against Valorians.

Lassen shot a glance back into his room—it was empty, but he could hear the commotion drawing nearer. The shuttle was as close as it could get, and Lassen jumped for the opening. One foot landed inside, but the other slipped and he lost his footing. An arm from inside the shuttle grabbed Lassen's and steadied him. A gold bracelet engraved with a sunburst circled the wrist of the arm that saved him. Lassen looked up into the triumphant face of Jihrmar, his cousin and advisor.

"May I see your travel pass?" Jihrmar joked above the tumult as he steadied Lassen, who was still somewhat shaken by his dramatic rescue.

"Sorry, I lost it in the gunfire!"

The agile Valorian completed the jump without trouble and the shuttle began to pull away from the building.

Just as the craft began to move, government center guards spilled into what was left of the guest room and opened fire.

Short blasts of energy blazed from their weapons. Only a few of the bolts made it through the hole and grazed the shuttle's hull. Jihrmar and the Valorian team returned the fire, but aiming was impossible as their craft raced away from the government center. Moments later the battle was over. One of the guards took one last shot at the now-distant vehicle and then in frustration threw his pistol into the broken glass, brick and charred wood.

"It is clear these dissident delegates are not only bent on disunity, they are bent on destruction as well," said Chairman Kruge, shaking his head. Shortly after Lassen's escape, he had gathered the delegates who had not signed the statement and they were discussing the evening's skirmish.

"Can we get them off the Council?" asked one delegate.

"There is no question about it," answered Kruge emphatically. "There is a clear provision in the charter for just such an occasion. We may even do so tonight; then I may appoint acting delegates I know will be more sensible. Although," added Kruge cryptically, "I think we should not replace Bolog, the delegate from Woodlander, just yet. We'll ask the others to leave Highland at dawn."

"I know Redland will not sit idly by while we appoint a replacement for their delegate," croaked the Highland delegate, a shriveled man who had to lean heavily on his staff just to sit up straight in his chair.

"True!" exclaimed Kruge. "That is why the Highland army is on full alert, performing manuevers in the cities and countryside at this moment. We must consider an international militia and police alliance to make sure these dissident nations do not rebel against the Council, especially Redland, with its vital energy resources."

Such a bold statement made even Kruge's loyal delegates uneasy. All were silent except for the Highland delegate who sucked on his lips and looked from person to person with his mattery eyes to see how his associates reacted. The Outerland delegate was claustrophobic to begin with, just being indoors and having to wear the extra clothes the cooler climate demanded—the current discussion of civil war drove him close to panic. The delegate from Shrilala buried her hands in the folds of her colorful wrappings and stared at the table.

Finally the old man of Highland rapped the Council table with his staff and declared, "Of course we must be prepared to do even that! Remember, we are going to have a new Vassir, a master planet! I think that this upset in the Council is timed by the gods to give us a chance to weed out the weak and the disloyal. Now is the perfect time to move. As a matter of fact, we should even station an army on Neece to make sure that settlement doesn't get any more insolent."

"The Highland delegate is right," said Kruge, more calmly now. "We must be prepared for this type of action. However, maybe a more diplomatic approach would be better, especially with Redland. I propose we send them a letter saying we understand their frightened response and that we still would like Lassen's *unofficial* input on the Council."

Again the delegates stared at Kruge, not understanding his last suggestion. The Highland delegate's wrinkled face folded in a silent grin as if Kruge had just told a private joke.

Lam and Lista stood near the back of the crowd that surrounded Neece's spaceport. Hundreds of people were there—just about the entire settlement—and Lam did not feel like being jostled.

"Who said Kruge was coming?" demanded Lista, trying to cover her fear with annoyance.

"I don't know where the information came from, but apparently everyone believes it," answered Lam with an edge to his voice. "If it's as reliable as the information I've been getting on Altua, he won't show."

"Look!" someone shouted. Hundreds of heads turned to search the sky. The murmurings grew louder as the dark specks above them grew larger. Soon five ships were visible, looming above them and looking larger as they descended.

"What's happening?" asked Lista, pulling on Lam's arm.

"There are five ships landing." Lam shielded his eyes has he studied the sky and narrated the unfolding drama for Lista. "They're not huge, but they're bigger than Starjumper. They seem new—highly polished. At first I thought they were black, but now I see they are dark red." Lam waited for the ships to get closer before continuing. By the time he took up his description for Lista again, he almost had to shout above the roar of the engines. "The first ones are landing. There is a symbol on each of them—a six-pointed star with two globes in front of it. That's the same symbol I saw in Kruge's speech. I guess there's no question who this is."

The throng quieted as it waited for the ships to complete landing. The last one settled on the pad by the others, a fierce cluster of warships standing silently like bombs waiting to explode.

Anxiety showed on nearly all faces. The sun was high and hot, and the press of hundreds of people who filled the grassy area around the port made it quite uncomfortable. Starting with the youngest, the crowd became restless waiting for the hatches to open. A few children, bored beyond their limits, chased each other through the crowd, followed by embarrassed parents who pleaded ineffectively with their offsprings. Random spectators now and then made muted comments to their neighbors, but for the most part, quiet suspense ruled the assembly.

Finally, in unison, the hatches of the ships hissed open. Dozens of soldiers dressed in red and black uniforms reinforced with armored breast and shoulder plates stormed from the ships with shoulder blasters readied in front of them. They marched down the gangway and formed several menacing columns between the crowd and the cluster of ships, then stood at attention while the sun glinted off the gold visors of their helmets.

After the soldiers had deployed, a figure emerged from the central ship. He also was dressed in red and black, but his clothes were civilian and sported a white sash. The crowd seemed to know the figure's identity, and moments after his appearance, cheering and applause began to swell.

Lam took advantage of a large layered rock rising above the ground next to him, climbed it, and shielded his eyes from the sun.

"It's Kruge all right," he called down to Lista over the commotion.

Chairman Kruge stood in the hatch of his ship and waved to the cheering crowd. A large, uncovered utility transport emerged from the port's only hangar and waited at the end of the stairs. Kruge descended and boarded the flatbed vehicle, still waving as the transport headed toward the crowd on its way to the main street of the settlement. The guards had no trouble keeping up with it as it slowly made its way. Some young men from the crowd climbed up the side of the spaceport station and tore down the banner of the Neecian settlement. Others snatched up the colorful flag and threw it onto the ground in front of Kruge's transport. The Chairman seemed quite pleased by the gesture.

Lam looked around at the faces of the crowd. There were all ages represented, but none seemed as happy as they sounded. Lam noticed that most of them eyed the soldiers with a veiled apprehension.

Once the troops and the boisterous masses turned down the path to the town, Lam and Lista were no longer out of the way. The press of people caught them up and they were pushed and jostled along so that they barely kept their balance. Lam held firmly onto Lista's hand so she wouldn't get swept away, but she stumbled several times despite his efforts.

Lam nearly panicked as the sweaty bodies pressed against his still-sore chest. He did some pushing of his own and managed to drag himself and Lista from the crush and onto the grass beside the path. Lam collapsed onto the ground and sat catching his breath while he watched the throng progress.

The annexation was swift. Lam and Lista, along with the entire settlement, heard Kruge's frenzied speech and the new laws. Soldiers hung the global Vassirian banner on the public buildings, and the Peace Enforcer's room became a distribution center for the flags that all private estates had to display as well.

"Lam, you don't know how horrible this is," Lista said, still in shock. They had listened to the new rules the Vassirians brought: control was absolute.

"It is an outrage," Lam agreed.

"It would be an outrage if it were anyone else taking over. This is disastrous!"

"Lista, you're trembling all over." Lam grasped her arm firmly and pulled her closer so that he could whisper. "I think you had better tell me what is so horrible about Highland—right now."

"Not here," Lista said, stifling a sob. "But I'll tell you."

"Let's get out of here, then. We have to get in touch with Me'Ben. If they're banning public meetings except for government rallies, our meeting with the Revered Ones is in trouble."

"If anyone catches us meeting with the Be'Nay," warned Lista darkly, "it will be more 'trouble.' "

Chapter Six

Lassen stood on a hill above the meadow outside Crystalia and reviewed the city that had sprung up overnight. Hundreds of grass-colored tents peppered the countryside. Black-armored Valorians and troops in camouflage fatigues swarmed in and out of them, carrying provisions and weapons. Personnel transports seemed to be arriving at the camp constantly, carrying more men ready to become soldiers.

A short distance from the camp, squads practiced their marksmanship. Lassen knew that a little ways from there, docked at the Crystalia spaceport, there were several small fighters, secretly salvaged from the Doomen when the Dominion fell. Jihrmar, in his foresight, had made their conversion to human use a top-priority project. They had completed the conversion and trained Valorians to fly them just shortly before the trouble with the Council of Delegates. He had hoped they would not have to be used against a Vassirian nation.

It frightened Lassen that it had come to this, but he was comforted knowing they were ready. He allowed himself one last look at the operation and then headed down the hill to the command tent.

Jihrmar and the squad leaders were waiting for him.

"What do you think our strategy should be?" asked Jihrmar when Lassen had joined them around the long table. Each man's face was determined, if not anxious. Lassen noted approvingly that his advisor and cousin, Jihrmar, no longer looked like an aristocratic Redlander, but wore camouflage fatigues, just like those troops and the squad leaders wore.

"The situation demands that we fortify our defenses as strongly and swiftly as possible," began Lassen gravely. "Chairman Kruge, as you know, has replaced me on the Council of Delegates. The other signers of the document Jihrmar told you about are probably also replaced by now—if not dead. The letter he sent informing us of the action amazed me—it sounded so understanding on the surface, but was so cruel underneath. The Chairman has assumed complete dictatorial control of Highland. Troops march the streets day and night, and his passionate rearming has produced some frightening weapons. He has also assumed complete control of Neece—possibly as many as five ships landed at their port and it is now a Vassirian, or should I say 'Highland,' colony instead of an independent settlement. Two or three Highland ships remain there to ensure their control."

Lassen stood up and stared out the tent flaps while he thought about how best to convey the weighty decision he had made. When he turned around, he spoke slowly and gravely.

"I have decided to cut off all shipments of Redlyn from my mine to Highland. To give him our precious resources is like feeding an unruly beast until it is strong enough to turn on its keeper. I know that he will consider attacking us to take by force what he needs and probably thinks is his."

Jihrmar slammed his hand on the table as an outlet for his anger against Kruge. Then he, too, rose to pace it off. He had suspected this would happen, but that had not altogether prepared him for it.

"Do you have any further information on Kruge's ambitions?" Jihrmar asked.

"My source desires to remain anonymous," Lassen answered for the squad leaders' sakes, "but he is very close to Chairman Kruge and has firsthand knowledge of the government-center operations. Unhappily, that also makes him difficult to contact in confidence. However"—Lassen paused to fish out the parchment Keneche gave him in the lobby of Kruge's study—"he asked me to contact him tonight by com-link reference."

The commander also rose and walked to the tent flaps.

"All this preparation is fine," said Jihrmar, joining Lassen in gazing at the busy camp. "We may be able to defend ourselves, but then again, it sounds like Highland has the weaponry advantage. We need to know his dealings with the other nations. We need to know the exact strength he possesses. We need to know if we have any allies." The counselor/commander gazed at Lassen piercingly.

"I'll contact the signers of the statement—Seaward, Sundor and Woodland—and I'll see who is willing to meet with us," Lassen announced resolutely. Jihrmar's face lightened a little.

"Let us hope they will speak to you after what has happened," Jihrmar joked. Then he added more soberly, "And there is one other thing to keep in mind. If the Chairman is as disturbed as he seems, perhaps we should make sure we never have to defend ourselves." The words had a chilling effect on Lassen.

"What do you mean, sir?" asked one of the squad leaders.

"He means our fighting may have to be something other than defensive," Lassen answered for Jihrmar.

"So, tell me!" Lam demanded of Lista. She started at the harsh words echoing off the damp, lantern-lit cave walls. Lam had been pacing in the sand, listening to the water drip from the cave ceiling as he waited for Lista to tell her story.

"You're going to start a cave-in!" she snapped back, still stalling.

"I'm sorry!" Lam sighed and sat down in the sand beside Lista and put his arm around her. "I really am," he said more gently. "I just wish you would trust me. As long as I've known you, you've acted tough to cover something up, and you haven't let me or anyone get too close to you. I'm tired of seeing you torn up that way."

"How are your ribs?"

Lam sighed in exasperation.

"They're fine—they just ache a little. I told you before, they were just bruised. Now, would you quit evading the subject?"

"It's just hard to talk about. I was raised in Woodland in a village called Travalia. Most of the continent called it 'the Crip Village.' Aba, the grandfather of the village, tells me I'm from Highland. I guess my parents didn't want a blind daughter. You see, it's been that way a long time."

"What's been what way?" Lam urged her on.

"Highlanders don't appreciate ethnic diversity—the Woodlanders are stupid, the Redlanders are greedy—you know. And
you have to be a perfect Highlander, too. They don't think much
of us crips."

"So the problem is they don't like people who are different
from themselves?" Lam asked.

"That was the problem up until a few years ago. My friends
in Travalia helped me get to Restoration Seminary in Highland.
That's where people study under the Restoration Masters to become Restorers. The very sick come to the seminary for healing,
but most Restorers work on their own in cities and villages. It
wasn't easy, but I made it through. I expected the taunting from
the other seminarians, and even the teachers. I expected to have
difficulty finding people to read me the books I needed to study,
but I wasn't prepared for what I learned there."

Lista paused and Lam hoped she would have the courage
to continue.

"For a long time the seminary taught that it was somehow
part of their duty to make Highland 'pure.' It took a while, but
I began to understand what that meant. It meant if a mother got
Herubena sickness when she was with child, the Restorer was
supposed to urge the mother to have a pre-birth separation—
you know, kill the tiny thing before he or she was born because
the baby would be deformed. It meant that if a baby was born a
crip like me, they would put it naked in an air vent until it died
from exposure."

Lista needed a chance to collect herself, so Lam just held
her firmly until she could begin again.

"That was just the beginning. A few Restorers have always
done those things, but the Restoration Masters started asking,
'What's so different about helping people die before they're
born, or when they're half dead anyway, and helping people die
when they're mentally sick, or a grown-up crip?' " She turned
to Lam and grasped his hand.

"Lam, imagine what this kind of thinking does to a man like
Kruge—think of the excuse he has for violence sanctioned by
Restoration Masters."

"Is it really that serious? Scholars say all kinds of absurd
things."

"Sometimes people forget that although I'm blind, I'm not deaf—I overhear things. And my few friends at the seminary told me things. I had friends who got caught up in this idea of overthrowing the Dominion, having Highland rule and purify Vassir and Neece. Kruge was their inspiration in the whole thing—that speech of his was well-rehearsed among his friends in Highland. Kruge is going to rule the solar system one way or another—just like he did when he was governor under the Dominion. And he's going to kill anyone he thinks he can blame for any troubles and anyone that gets in his way."

"Like the Be'Nay and the people in your village," Lam said softly, stunned by her story.

"Like me."

"You came to Neece to run from that, didn't you?" Lam said as gently as he could. Lista nodded somberly.

"Now that I see he's gone this far," Lista added, "I'm really beginning to worry about my friends in Travalia—they are the closest I've ever had to family."

"There must be a way to stop him!" Lam exclaimed, rising to his feet. "He's probably responsible for Altua's disappearance, too. But first, when Me'Ben comes, we'll arrange a time to meet with the Revered Ones."

"You can't go through with that meeting now! It's completely illegal—didn't you hear the new laws?"

"Listen, I can handle these slime eaters—" Lam started angrily.

"And when you meet with the Revered Ones," demanded Lista, "what will you tell them? How much peace comes from the Way of Tsu? How great it is to have a Friend who takes care of you?"

Lam reeled around to confront Lista. He was furious at everything—even her, a little. But he couldn't say anything. He knew she was right. He stood helplessly, not caring that icy water dripped on his head and ran down his neck. *When did the Source abandon me?* he wondered. He had not really noticed it until now, although he had known something was wrong for a long time.

"Lam," pleaded Lista, "say something to me." The edge

had left her voice and she sounded very alone. Hearing her that way, and feeling the way he did, he didn't know whether to rage at the Source or turn away and let his emotions escape. He did neither, only stood.

"I'm sorry, I didn't mean that," Lista said quietly and sadly. A tear trailed down her face before she could brush it away.

"Mesha, Sarin," greeted Me'Ben, stepping in from a darkened entrance to the cavern room Lam had lit with a lantern. Both Lam and Lista, glad for the distraction from their troubles, hurried to meet him.

"Are you aware that Chairman Kruge of Vassir has taken over this planet?" Lam inquired, brushing aside the pleasantries.

"He has taken over the Vassirian settlers, not the Be'Nay," said the native dryly.

"Then you are aware of his laws forbidding meetings?" asked Lam.

"We are aware of these things. It is the position of the Revered Ones that—"

"I know, I know," Lam cut him off, "that 'this trouble will pass in time as have all the troubles.' But this time is different. The Dominion did not care about you and so they left you alone—these Vassirians hate you!"

"Not all Vassirians," added Lista, putting her hand on Me'Ben's shoulder.

Me'Ben smiled at her in thanks, but his expression quickly changed.

"Someone is coming!" Me'Ben warned in a whisper. Lam reached for the lantern, and Me'Ben grabbed Lista's arm, ready to lead her out another direction in the maze of caves the Be'Nay of that area knew well.

"Halt!" ordered the Peace Enforcer, lumbering awkwardly into the cave. "Come out now, and no one will be hurt!" Lam would not have counted him a threat if he had been alone, but two Vassirian soldiers burst into the cave behind the pathetic Enforcer.

Without thinking, Lam reached for his Redlyn pistol. He grasped it and swung it toward the intruders. The Peace Enforcer dropped his bulk to the ground and readied his own weapon.

The soldiers dove behind rocks and loosed blinding red bolts from their military pistols. Whines filled the room. Lam jumped backward to get out of the way and pulled Lista to the ground.

"Mesha, Sarin!"

Lam turned briefly to see Me'Ben standing near an opening into a different chamber, motioning frantically for them to follow him.

The blaster bolts ripped into the rock walls and sprayed chips of stone across the cave before the echoes of the volley slowly died. Lam twisted where he lay and saw Lista lying motionless on the ground beside him. He turned the other way and saw with horror that Me'Ben was sprawled on the sand with a red gash in his side. His eyes stared upward.

"No!" shouted Lam at the top of his lungs until his throat burned. *This is my fault! Did I think I could save us all with some fancy shooting? Now look!* he accused himself, but he could only shout, "No!"

Lassen watched the outcast Council delegates mill about in the starlit solarium of his house in Crystalia. He managed to convince all of the signers to meet him there—it seemed he was not the only one afraid of what Kruge might do next. Siah was there, the former delegate from Seaward. The ousted delegate from Sundor was there too, wearing his white skirt and turban. And Bolog.

Bolog was the delegate from Woodland and was one of the reasons Lassen had not enjoyed being a delegate more. It was not that the heavy-set man was unkind, just obnoxious. Bolog's tunic barely contained his belly, and each of his fat fingers supported one or two jeweled rings. Precious metal chains hung around his almost nonexistent neck.

"What are you doing lurking in the dark, Redlander?" bellowed Bolog. Lassen took a deep breath and entered the room to join the others.

"I don't know what the fuss is about. Why doesn't Redland just buy Highland?" chided Bolog, jabbing his elbow into Lassen's side. But Lassen was tired of jokes about Redland's supposed riches.

"Woodland can help; it certainly has wealth enough to feed its delegates well," said Lassen, applying his own elbow to Bolog's stomach.

"We have business here, boys," Siah reminded them. She alighted on a chair and gestured to the empty seats that faced her in the circle.

The others joined her and after Lam introduced Jihrmar, they discussed the situation as each of them perceived it.

"The question before us is, 'What do we do about this?' " Lassen pointed out.

"What if all our nations get together and send a delegation?" insisted Bolog finally. "Surely then he would listen to reason!"

"I assure you there is no reasoning with him," asserted Lassen. "And my contact in Wyntir has watched him regularly. Kruge has not slept well for many days. He is angry and agitated. If ever there were a chance to reach him with reason, it is long past."

"I frankly don't know any way to deal with him but by force," said Siah sternly. "As long as he is alive, we are not safe."

Bolog leapt from his chair.

"What you are suggesting is assassination!" he fumed. "I'll have no part in that! I say we send a delegation. I'll lead it myself if the rest of you are afraid."

It was too late to continue much longer, so the group decided to accept Bolog's offer. No one but Bolog was convinced it would be successful, but they reasoned that no one could fault them if they sought peaceful solutions first.

After the crowd filtered out of his room, Lassen turned to Jihrmar.

"An interesting gathering," said Lassen. "They sounded as if they had a hard time believing the things that Keneche told me."

"You only told them half of the things we found out from the boy."

"I didn't want to jeapordize Keneche's identity—he's in a sensitive position."

"He's in an explosive position."

"I feel sorry for him. He's too young to feel responsible for the fates of seven nations. And I am reasonably certain that his mother is Cruzan's daughter, and as far as we know, Cruzan and his daughter are still missing."

"Do you think he's worried about Cruzan?" Jihrmar asked. "After all, he is the Valorian Master. Valorians may owe allegiance to their own countries, but they all respect the Master—he's capable of taking care of himself, and he has the world's Valorians on his side."

"I don't know what's going on in the boy's head. That's another reason I hesitated telling more to our guests tonight—much of what he told us is only rumor and Chairman Kruge would deny it, anyway. Like the stories of government-center staff fleeing Highland in the middle of the night because they're afraid of being beaten. Who can say how much of that is really going on?"

"Still, I don't know what Bolog hopes to gain with this delegation of his," Jihrmar responded, shaking his head.

"I don't blame him for wanting to solve this peacefully," Lassen offered.

"There's no peace," spat Jihrmar. "The battle lines are already drawn, the weapons readied, and the passions raised. There is no peace—only waiting."

Lassen shuddered. "I hope you are wrong," he said, shaking his head.

"I wish I were."

Chapter Seven

Lam slammed his hand against the metal door of his cell. As he paced, he thought about his interrogation—they had demanded that he tell them what he knew about Kruge, about Altua, about other things he had never heard of. And he had gotten Me'Ben killed because of his stupid attempt to shoot it out. And Lista— he had no idea how badly she might have been hurt! *Kruge—I hate him!* Lam thought, slamming his fist against the door again.

He was exhausted from the ordeal of the fight, the capture, and the interrogation. He had completely lost track of time, but he guessed that at least one day had passed. He could tell by an air slot to the outside that it was night. He again looked out the tiny window in his door to the hallway. As always, it revealed nothing, only the guard standing at attention halfway down the hall. He was hoping for at least a glimpse of Lista—he was not even sure if she was dead or alive.

"Hey, guard!" Lam called. "Have you ever killed anyone?" The man did not respond. "I have," he continued, "several, in fact. Never in cold blood, though. I was a pirate, you know. I attacked Dominion supply ships and killed anyone who tried to stop me."

Reason seeped back into Lam's mind and he realized the interrogation had broken down most of his internal defenses. His violent past flooded back to him.

Even after I met the Friend, I had those deaths pushed out of my mind, Lam realized. *I don't blame the Source for keeping his distance.*

"It's Me'Ben that's bringing it all back to me," Lam muttered to himself. "Altua's probably dead too by now. Lista, I pray that you're all right at least."

Lam hung on the door to keep his weary legs from collapsing

and looked through the screen. A white haze began to creep into the hall and Lam watched through the screen as tentrils of smoke wound their way along the floor and curled around the guard's leg. Lam waited for the man to call "fire" and run for help, but he didn't move, he just stared straight ahead as if he were in a trance.

As the vapor reached Lam's cell, the pungent fumes stung his nostrils. He saw the guard slump to the floor against the wall. But before Lam had a chance to wonder what had happened, he became dizzy and lost his grip on the door. He put out his hands to catch his fall, but was unconscious before he hit the floor, unaware of the electronic key being held to the scanner button on his door or the door of his cell swinging open.

Bolog, the delegate from Woodland, did not find many volunteers for his mission to the government center. He traveled in a shuttle filled with half a dozen dignitaries from Woodland and one each from Redland, Seaward, and Sundor.

"Chairman Kruge is expecting us, then?" demanded a worried elderly Woodlander seated next to Bolog and clutching the arms of his seat.

"Yes, he is," bellowed Bolog. "And I promise that there is nothing to fret about." That shut up the worrier for the moment, although it did not seem to comfort him.

"Strap in, everyone. We are beginning our descent to Wyntir Interstellar Port," announced the pilot over the voicecaster.

The cabin lights dimmed as the shuttle diverted power to the gravity resistors. Bolog leaned back in his seat, and taking advantage of the subdued lighting smiled slyly.

They were met at the port by a covered transport from the government center. The attendants efficiently loaded the delegation in, and the transport rose from the ground and sped off toward their meeting with Kruge.

Their reception at the government center was equally efficient. They were unloaded, attendants swept away their luggage and several guards escorted them to the hall where they assumed they would meet Kruge. All the while, Bolog hung back and watched the proceeding with a grim amusement.

The group marched down the flag-lined hallway, ten pairs of feet creating quite a din as they walked. Some had not been in the center before, and looked admiringly at the stone work and crystal chandeliers. They soon reached a double gate of black metal wrought into amazingly intricate patterns of climbing plants and flowers. Those who had been there before stood looking confused as the guards swung open the gates and gestured them in. This was no meeting room; it was a banquet hall, and they could all see the long elegantly set table. A tapestry tablecloth was draped over the finely carved tabletop. Expensive dishes and crystal adorned the table, and a feast of fruit and delicacies was spread across the length of it.

The delegation wandered in wide-eyed, and Bolog leaned back and bounced his belly in a hearty laugh at the reaction of his comrades.

"Welcome, honored guests!" called Chairman Kruge, strolling in from a door on the opposite side of the hall. "It is good to see you—I have been looking forward to your company." He motioned for them all to sit down and called for servants to pour the drink.

Such a feast would have been wildly delightful for the guests—except that they kept looking at Kruge and Bolog as they sat together in the middle. *They will eventually broach the subject of the meeting*, everyone thought, but it never happened. Bolog, however, was quite content. He knew there would be no such discussions—the events had been carefully planned.

The decorative lamps on the table were nearly out of oil before Bolog rose and addressed the delegation.

"I hope you have all enjoyed yourselves this night," he said. Nodding heads and patted stomachs affirmed that they had. "Good, good. This is the way honored guests are treated here at the government center. I am asking that each of you stay on for a few days as guests of Chairman Kruge. I know you will enjoy your visit, and you will be doing Woodland, not to mention Vassir, a great service. Are there any objections?"

No one voiced their objections, but anxiety was apparent on each face.

"Good!" Bolog commended. "Your rooms are ready for you.

Enjoy your night's sleep—and have a wonderful time here!"

As the last of the Woodlanders followed his attendant out of the hall, Kruge commended, "You certainly picked a cooperative company, Bolog."

"Thank you, Chairman. But who could object to your hospitality?" The two laughed.

"Tell me," said Bolog in a less boisterous tone. "I have been wondering what ever happened to the Tsuian fellow?"

"Altua?"

"Yes, that's the one."

"Last I heard, he was still hanging on. I thought he would be dead long ago."

"I feel bad that he has to suffer so much," pouted Bolog.

"Try not to worry about it," Kruge comforted him. "It is for the glory of the new Vassir, remember? Here, have another drink."

When Lam began sorting out reality from the strange dreams he had been having, he heard a woman's voice say, "I think he's coming out of it."

"You are right, Mesha," a deep, familiar voice responded.

Lam forced open his eyes and blinked them into focus. He found himself lying beside a campfire in the dark, with Lista and Me'Ben on either side of him. The fire gave her skin a reddish glow and sparkled in the reflection of her finder. Me'Ben had a crude bandage of torn cloth wrapped around his chest. Beside Me'Ben was Lam's pistol. He pushed himself up on his elbow and a stick snapped under his weight.

"Welcome to the land of the conscious," kidded Lista.

"Thanks, but it seems to me this is not where I went to sleep," groaned Lam, trying to sit up.

"You and I were both locked up at the Peace Enforcer's office, remember?" prodded Lista.

"Yes, I remember that, but I don't remember leaving."

"Me'Ben and his friends broke us out."

"They what?"

"It was simple, Sarin," Me'Ben explained. He pulled out a handful of fungus fragments from a pouch that hung around his waist and showed them to Lam. "When these burn, it makes what we call 'sleeping smoke.' It let us carry you and Mesha out under the guard's snoring noses. We also got your pistol."

" 'Sleeping smoke,' you call it? Strong stuff," Lam admitted, rubbing his eyes. "But I thought you weren't supposed to get involved in all this. Did you go against the Revered Ones?"

"No!" gasped Me'Ben. "We postponed their wishes to accomplish this."

"I'm grateful," Lam said. "I'm also relieved to see you are alive."

"As far as the officials of New Highland are concerned, I am dead. It is a trick we learn from the forest animals."

Me'Ben lowered his voice and continued almost guiltily, "I helped you because you're my friends, but also because I want you to do something about this sickness of violence the Highlanders of Vassir are bringing. You and Mesha Lista are not under vows to the Revered Ones as I am."

Lam looked at Lista who seemed touched by the Neecian's plea. Lam did not feel quite up to destroying another dictatorship, but he felt compelled to become involved somehow. Even before all this had happened, Lam had decided that Altua, if he was still live, was probably on Vassir, and that Kruge had something to do with his disappearance. The mission that drove him to search for the elderly ambassador seemed to be taking on cosmic proportions.

"While you were sleeping off the fungus, I decided something," Lista said quietly, leaning closer to Lam. "It's no safer here than on Vassir, anyway. I have to go to Travalia, my home on Vassir, and warn them about Kruge and the Highlanders and help them if I can." Her voice was shaky, and Lam suspected that her decision was difficult. "I have to do it for me, if no one else," she added almost inaudibly.

Lam let her words sink in. Lista wanted to go to Vassir— out of the sunspot and into the sun, probably. Lista's decision forced Lam to consider his own future. He was wanted by the Vassirian government now, and as Lam saw it, he had three choices. He could remain a fugitive on Neece the rest of his life, living in the woods with the Be'Nay—if they'd let him. Or, he could return to Tsu, with no news of Altua, defeated, beaten, and bitter. Or—he sighed deeply to relieve the tension as he thought about it—he could ignore the risk and go to Vassir with Lista to continue his search there. Lista needed him and his ship to make it to her home village, and, he realized, he needed her. Somehow even the pain they'd suffered together drew him to her.

"You're not going unless you take me," Lam finally said, not sounding very stern. Lista smiled and wrapped her arms around him. Her embrace hurt his ribs a little, but it made their situation seem a little less desperate.

When Lista finally let go, she sat back on the ground and asked excitedly, "Me'Ben, do you think you can get us into the port so we can get to Starjumper?"

Me'Ben smiled. "What the Be'Nay attempt, we accomplish."

Lassen's wife sat down on the edge of the sleeping couch where Lassen reclined. She had just said good night to the last of their brood of six and joined her husband in their own room.

"I don't think you should trust the Woodlander," she advised him. They had been discussing the delegation before the children's sleep time, and she took it up again as she sat next to Lassen.

"Bolog?"

"Yes, I don't think you should trust him—at least don't depend on him."

"Why not?" asked Lassen, amused at his wife's sudden advice.

"How many wives does he have?"

Lassen thought for a moment. "Three—or maybe four."

"See? Any man who cannot choose the right woman for himself the first time cannot be trusted." She leaned over and kissed her husband on the nose.

"I never did like the man much," Lassen admitted.

"You may laugh now, but remember my words," she warned, slipping under the covers.

"It is hard to know whom to trust and what to depend on

these days," Lassen sighed as he touched the light beside the sleeping couch to dim it. "All I know is that what Bolog tells us when he returns will determine whether Redland will be part of the Master Planet, or whether we will be at war."

Chapter Eight

All but one of Neece's moons had set, and a sheet of clouds muted even its light. It was much too late for anyone to be awake except the Highland soldiers on watch around their warships at the port.

The floodlights were an artificial intrusion into the night, welcomed only by the soldier making his rounds and the insects that hurled themselves at the lights, only to be incinerated by the heat. Through this darkness, three figures crept out of the woods toward the guardhouse at the perimeter of the spaceport.

One of the figures ran low to the ground and pressed himself like a shadow against the guardhouse. The second figure made it to a post containing a wiring box for the glaring lights. Me'Ben, the guardhouse's assailant, reached into his pockets and fished out a handful of fungus. He placed it into a bowl and added two drops of liquid from either end of a small vial. Smoke immediately began to billow from the bowl and Me'Ben lifted it to the house's open window. The same opening that had drawn in fresh air to help the sentinel keep awake now drew in the vapors.

A thud told Me'Ben that the guard had succumbed. He gestured at Lam who drew his Redlyn pistol from his belt and took careful aim at the box. There was one red flash, and then darkness.

Lista ran from her cover to join Lam. They heard several surprised and angry shouts from the far end of the port. Lam could tell the patrol was shouting about switching on back-up lights.

"Hurry, Lista," he whispered, needlessly anxious. With her finder, Lista could navigate the darkness much better than he.

In a moment, he heard her footfalls and rapid breathing. "Lead the way!" he told her.

Lista was in her element—total darkness. She had activated her finder and led Lam through the port toward Starjumper.

It won't be long until they get those lights on, Lam warned himself as he tried to keep from tripping over his own feet in the darkness and listened to the shouting getting closer. *Just a little longer—in the name of the Friend, just a little longer!*

"We're almost there," Lista announced between gulps of air. Before her words barely had a chance to register, Lam was blinded by light. Lista was still holding his hand, pulling him toward Starjumper.

"They found lights!" Lam called to her.

"Have they found *us*?"

Lam looked around him as he ran. The lights had not yet betrayed them, but their beams danced across the pavement looking for the perpetrators of the blackout.

"Not yet—keep running!" Lam urged.

Suddenly one of the blinding beams landed on them. Lam froze and looked up into it, but Lista kept running toward Starjumper. He'd been caught. *Don't give up,* something urged. Lam shook himself, raised his pistol and shot at the light. After a spray of sparks, it went dark. The other beam searched for him, but Lam had already sprinted for his ship, now just a few strides away.

"Stop!" ordered a Highland soldier, now pursuing Lam on foot. When Lam did not stop, the soldier aimed his pistol. Anticipating fire, Lam zigzagged to make a more difficult target. Several rounds tore past his head and vanished into the night— one glanced off the hull of Starjumper.

Lam swung around and returned the fire, but dared not take time to take aim. Again the soldier shot at him, but Lam was almost to Starjumper's stairs. Lam spun around to fire at his pursuer as he ran, but before he could pull the activator twice, he bumped into Starjumper's diamond wing with his bruised side. He fell to his knees in agony.

He forced himself to his feet and grabbed the stair railing, then he was on board without touching more than two of the steps.

"Close the hatch!" Lam yelled, tumbling onto Starjumper's deck. Lista had already found the hatch button and was waiting to push it. It hissed closed after Lam, and they heard the bolts, intended for Lam, scream in protest as they glanced off the gleaming hull.

Scrambling to the pilot's seat, Lam pressed one panel after the other in furious speed.

"Strap in!" Lam commanded as he grasped the controls in his hand and pulled back. Lam saw red bolts from Redlyn pistols piercing the night sky through his viewing screen as the whine from Starjumper's engines gained intensity. Lista found a seat and fumbled for the harness. The engines had barely reached propulsion rate when Lam jerked the vertical thrust bar. With fierce power, the craft shot upward, slamming Lam and Lista into their seats.

Bolog seemed quite agitated when Lassen met him at Crystalia's port.

"I'm surprised he let me go," Bolog fumed. "He almost didn't—the rest of our people are still there as hostages! Kruge ranted like a madman when we brought up our concerns to him."

Lassen shook his head in dismay.

"He demanded to know the names of the other 'conspirators.' Can you believe he called us that? Why, in his ranting he even hinted that he was going to be *the* global power!"

Lassen ushered the irate Woodlander into his personal transport and continued listening as they sped toward Lassen's compound. The roomy vehicle was enclosed in a bubble of darkened crystal, unlike utility transports which had only flatbeds, and the smooth ride seemed to calm Bolog a bit.

"You know, listening to that madman, I believe he is going to try some sort of takeover," Bolog confided in Lassen. "And you know what nation will be first on his list, don't you?"

"The one with the Redlyn," growled Lassen. Although he had expected the worst of the mission, he had to admit he hadn't been prepared for the news Bolog brought.

"You know, Redlander," Bolog said, leaning his bulk toward

Lassen and speaking in an exaggerated whisper, "I don't see that we have any other choice. We have to ally our armies and strike while we have surprise on our side."

"*You* are suggesting we attack Highland?" asked Lassen, amazed at the change in his companion's attitude of several nights before.

"Shh!" urged Bolog, although no one but Lassen's private driver could possibly hear them. "I know it sounds crazy, but listen, I was shaken up. It's him or us!"

So this is the answer we have been waiting for, Lassen realized. *War.*

"What are they?" asked Lista. Although she could not see the red spots around the image of Vassir on Starjumper's viewing screen, she could hear the blips as the detection beams bounced back off the objects and returned to Starjumper's instruments for analysis.

"Satellites," said Lam, pulling on his chin. "In Kruge's Master Planet speech, he talked about rearming to prevent another invasion. I suppose these are defense satellites. There's a string of them around the entire planet."

To avoid flying into a snare, they had decided against using the light gates. The journey was longer that way, but it gave Lam and Lista some desperately needed rest. Lam spent much of the trip dozing in the pilot's seat while Lista slept buckled into the bunk in back. Now they were nearly in orbital range of her home planet, and the glow of the instrument panel illuminated the disappointment on their faces.

"I was afraid it wouldn't be easy," confessed Lam.

"We won't get through unless we're invited," sighed Lista.

Lam leaned back in his seat, closed his eyes and thought. He had learned many tricks during his years with the pirate Cartel, and now he reviewed them.

"There are basically three ways to break a defense system," Lam thought out loud. "Bribery, force, and deceit."

"Oh, and I'm an expert at all of them," said Lista.

"We have no valuables for a bribe. We are certainly no match for a ring of armed satellites. That leaves deceit."

Lam sat upright in his seat and swung it to face Lista who was in the seat next to him.

"Who normally travels to Vassir?" asked Lam.

"Well, mostly merchant vessels and supply ships."

"We wouldn't pass as either of those—we don't have any merchandise or supplies."

"Shuttles from Neece," continued Lista, ransacking her mind, "and shuttles from the moon base on Elna. Those both run pretty often."

Lam's eyebrows raised at Lista's last statement.

"I think our best bet is to stow away on a moon-base shuttle."

"What? That happens to be a military base!" exclaimed Lista.

Lam explained his plan on the way to Elna's dark side. By the time he settled Starjumper into the dust, he almost had Lista convinced that they stood a chance. He still had to convince himself.

"Put this helmet on," Lam coached as Lista struggled with the pressure suit.

"Don't rush me. I think this thing is wrestling me, and it's twice as big as I am."

"There, I knew you could do it. Now, remember, the suit seals minor rips by itself. The oxygen flow is regulated by this dial on your belt, and we should avoid using the com-links in case the base uses this frequency."

"Great. I can't see and you won't talk to me. I don't suppose my finder will work through this helmet, either."

"I suppose not, but somehow I think you'll do fine." Lam gave her a peck on the cheek before he helped her lower her helmet and seal it to the suit. Lam pressed the hatch, and the rear compartment hissed in protest as its air was sucked out into the near-vacuum of Vassir's moon. He threw back the flap on the saddlebag that hung over the skip's seat for one last check. It contained food and water and other provisions that would not be useful until they were back in air. It contained two extra oxygen canisters, which he hoped they wouldn't need, and random tools lined in the side pockets. He had also placed the M-stone amulet and the tri-cornered leaf rock from the Le-in. He didn't know when he would be able to return to Starjumper, and he didn't know when he might need the comfort of those trinkets.

Lam then boosted Lista onto Starjumper's skip, a small white vehicle just big enough for two. He swung onto the long, narrow seat so that he sat in front of Lista and slipped his hands into the control gloves. When he flexed his fingers, sensors in the gloves took direction and the motor whirred to life.

Lam activated the gravity resistors and they gently lifted from the deck. He made sure Lista was holding on tight; then he pulled back and the two of them shot out of the hatch and plummeted to the ground, stopping just above the dust. The vehicle sped away from Starjumper and toward the base. Their plan was still a little hazy, but Lam claimed he knew every possible hiding place on a ship, and how to get to it—they should have no problem stowing away. For now all Lam could do was enjoy the narrow band of rocky landscape lit by their skip's headlamp. All Lista could do was enjoy the quiet.

Lam purposely chose a flat area so that their course would be straight and uneventful. The most interesting scenery they passed were rock outcroppings and tumbles of stones that had been thrown up by small meteor impacts. The only major obstacle was a low ridge still a ways off that Lam had spotted on Starjumper's viewing screen—he hoped there would be a pass through it.

With no air resistance, the skip traveled faster than Lam was used to, and at times he would have to slow down to regain tenuous control of his driving. Lista just silently clung to Lam's waist and hoped he knew what he was doing. Lam began to wonder himself until he finally spotted the ridge.

Lam squinted and tried to judge the distance to the ridge. He could barely make out the crest, but they were still too far from Lam to see if there was an easy pass.

As Lista feared, Lam was driving too fast—on Elna, he didn't even have air to hold him back. She wanted to protest, but he had ordered com-link silence. If he had been driving slower, or watching his route instead of the ridge, they might have avoided the boulder,

The rock, half embedded in the dusty moon soil, was just high enough to scrape the bottom of their skip. Lam felt the impact and pulled up, but overcompensated—and at their speed, he couldn't recover control fast enough. The skip flipped and threw both of them from the seat. The craft hit the ground and tumbled like a weed blown by a breeze until it reached a pile of rocks that had been strewn there from some meteor impact ages ago. The runaway skip crashed into the stone and dislodged a miniature avalanche; in moments, it was crushed and half buried.

"Lista?" Lam called into his com-link.

"I'm here, and that's the last time I'm riding one of those things with you." Lam heard her voice crackle in the com-link. Their landing was rough, but they had escaped the fate of their skip.

"I thought we weren't supposed to use the com-link," Lista complained.

"We have more to worry about than that. We have nearly a full day's walk ahead of us, no light, and barely enough oxygen."

By then Lam's eyes had adjusted to the red glow and he could faintly see the outline of Lista's suit lying on the ground not far from him. He pushed himself up, walked stiffly to Lista and helped her up.

"Which way?" asked Lista. Lam shrugged.

"I think it's that way, but the compass was on the skip."

The two stood in the near-darkness and reflected on their predicament.

"This is about as serious as it gets, isn't it?" Lista remarked.

"I'm afraid so," replied Lam, a little shakily.

"Lam, both you and Altua talked about how powerful the Source is, and how the Power guides his followers. And you talked about how the Friend is always there ready to act on our behalf."

"Yes, Lista," Lam agreed, impressed by her summary. He was not sure she had taken it all in—and afraid that she had probably rejected it because of the way he had been acting.

"If there are any other gods, none live up here. Please talk to your Friend and see if he will help us."

"I hope he remembers me," Lam said beneath his breath. He closed his eyes and was startled when it made little difference—it was almost as dark with his eyes open. The Friend felt far away, and Lam felt foolish as he probed his mind, which seemed as dark as the moon.

Lam felt stupid and inept. He was reasonably sure that the Source had lost patience with him and left. That thought made him suddenly realize how alone they were, and how hostile their host world.

"I'm sorry, Lista," Lam said quietly.

"For what?" asked Lista, touched by the pain in his voice.

"I must be miserable company. I'm sorry for telling you about the Friend and then forgetting about it. I wanted you to know him. Now, what if it's too late?"

Lista put her arms around him as best she could and tried to comfort him.

"You're right, you have been a pain. But we're just wasting oxygen talking about it now."

Lam pushed himself away from her, nodded his agreement and walked to the remains of their skip. The rear of the skip protruded from the debris, so he fished the saddlebag from the dust and tugged Lista's arm in the direction they had been headed before the crash. They began their trek to the moon base.

Chapter Nine

Even before the oxygen began to run out, Lam was miserable. The pressure suits were not made for long excursions—they had no way to relieve their thirst or take care of any other physical need. At least the minimal gravity meant that each stride took them twice as far as they would go under normal conditions on Vassir.

The stars did not provide enough illumination to keep them from tripping over stones that littered the dusty surface of the moon, and Lam constantly feared that he would be completing one of his flying strides right against the face of a stone wall.

"Let's stop here for a moment," Lam said as Lista bounded up behind him. "I can't see the terrain any better than you can, but I'm beginning to know how it feels. As near as I can tell by the stars, if I've remembered how this satellite spins, we're headed in the right direction."

Lam was looking up at the stars when the dizziness first hit him. He stumbled to keep his balance, but found himself sliding down the face of a cliff. The slow-motion effect of the low gravity only prolonged the agony of his fall.

"Lam! What's happening?" Lista called into her com-link. The only answer she received was Lam's grunts of pain. She dropped to her knees and crawled cautiously to where she believed Lam last stood and in moments felt the lip of the cliff from which he had fallen.

"Be careful," Lista heard her comrade order weakly.

"I'm all right—what about you?" Lista answered.

"I've just about used up my oxygen."

Lista noticed the staleness of her own air.

"Lam! What will we do?"

"When I fell, I dropped the saddlebag with the extra oxygen," Lam panted. "I can't find it!"

"I wish my finder worked through this stupid helmet," Lista agonized. She lowered herself over the edge and let herself slide down, in much better control than Lam's descent.

"I'm feeling for it too, Lam. How much longer can we go without it?"

His response was slow and slurred.

"If I see you again, I guess we'll both know that the Friend cares."

"Lam!" gasped Lista, starting to feel dizzy now herself.

"I'd hate not to see you again," said Lam deliriously. Then there was no more sound from his com-link. Lista pulled herself along the ground, swinging her arms looking for him. She felt that if she could only be near him, everything would be all right. She groped along the ground, hoping to feel his pressure suit, but instead all she felt was rocks—until she felt the rail.

What is this? she wondered to herself. She decided that it could be a carbon-dioxide-poisoning illusion, but it certainly felt like a metal rail imbedded in the ground. Lista was too light-headed to imagine what significance it had. It was just something to interest her while she suffocated. Just one more sensation, like the burning in her lungs.

She did not have much of a chance to contemplate her discovery. She slowly let herself down and rested her head against the track. She did not feel the vibrations in the rail. In the distance, a small but growing light pierced the darkness. Lam regained consciousness for a fleeting moment and saw the light coming. He had heard somewhere that death was like approaching a bright light.

"Your interference must have been from a sun flare or something," the driver of the rail transport vehicle heard his partner say over the com-link. Their features were not distinguishable beneath their pressure suits. The suits themselves were a dark red and on the right arms there were hexagrams with two globes superimposed over them.

"No, I don't think so—I could have sworn I heard voices in

my com-link," the driver argued.

"The dark side of the moon does that to a person sometimes," mocked the other. Suddenly he felt the small vehicle lurch as the driver braked it.

"Look at that," the driver said, pointing ahead of them. "Do you think I'm imagining things now?"

They had stopped just short of Lista's body lying against the track. Lam's could be seen just at the edge of their headlamp's beam.

"Quick, get the spare oxygen!" the driver's partner ordered as he jumped out of the vehicle, pistol drawn, to aid the fallen strangers.

Lam had expected to wake up on the Other Side, but instead he woke up in a stark room decorated only with a portrait of Chairman Kruge.

"I'm not on the Other Side, that's for sure," he muttered after seeing the Chairman's image. He rubbed his eyes, yawned and pushed himself up from his bed. There was not much else to see. His pistol and everything else he had been carrying was gone. His room was furnished with a washbasin and a relief basin, which he quickly made use of. He splashed the cool water on his face and rubbed it with a towel that hung nearby. When he turned, he noticed that a tiny light on a gray box above the door was blinking.

A motion detector, thought Lam. This observation was confirmed when the door swung open to reveal a Vassirian in a dark red jumpsuit, the kind used for wearing beneath pressure suits. The Vassirian brandished a large, military-style Redlyn pistol and sternly ordered Lam to do something, but he could not understand the man. Lam knew by the hexagram emblem on his arm that he was Vassirian and probably spoke one of their dialects.

"I'm sorry," said Lam in Common. "Could you repeat that?"

"Come with me," the guard said in the more universally understood tongue, annoyed with having to repeat himself. "I'm taking you to see the base commander, Brakan."

Now I at least know where we are, thought Lam as he followed his guide into the narrow hallway. *We . . .* That reminded Lam, *Where is Lista?*

"I was with a woman," began Lam.

"Brakan will answer your questions," Lam's escort curtly replied.

As they trekked the narrow, white halls, Lam wondered how the moon-base personnel kept from going insane in the confined spaces. When the guard knocked and then swung open the door to Brakan's cabin, Lam saw how.

Lam's escort led him into a spacious suite of rooms. One wall was entirely glass and behind it was a lush indoor garden. Trees, flowers and foliage crowded together in an attractive display around a pond with a brightly colored lizard creeping along the edge. There were even a couple of songbirds chirping in the branches of the trees.

The walls, along with a few display stands, sported a few art treasures and some of Brakan's awards and decorations. The room in which they were standing had two molded white chairs and a molded white couch, each with blue cushions that matched the carpeting.

"So this is our unfortunate visitor!" Lam turned at the sound of the deep, strong voice. From the way the man walked into the room, and by the decorations on his uniform, Lam knew that this was Brakan.

"A much more fortunate visitor than I expected to be a short time ago," responded Lam. Brakan laughed heartily as he grasped Lam's forearm and introduced himself.

"And you're Lam Laeo," Brakan said, saving Lam from the decision to remain anonymous. "Somehow involved in the fall of the Dominion. Sometimes merchant, all the time trouble-maker."

"Where's Lista?" demanded Lam, a little more forcefully than he would have if he had not been insulted. Brakan gestured to the door through which Lista was just being ushered. She had a frightened but determined look on her face.

"Lista!" Lam exclaimed, running to meet her. Lista's face suddenly turned to one of intense joy, and she bit her lip as she returned Lam's embrace.

"Thank the Source you're all right," she whispered.

"We're all right so far," Lam agreed warmly.

"Isn't this touching?" cooed Brakan, clapping his hands together. "Please, sit down," he insisted, motioning to the seats. As Lista and Lam sat down, Brakan motioned the soldier to leave. The door closed behind him.

"Well," began Brakan, "how do you happen to be wandering the dark side of our fair moon?"

"If you know who we are, you probably know."

"You're right." Brakan's bushy white sideburns puffed out a little has he grinned. "I have a pretty good idea." He leaned back and studied his guests with intense blue eyes. Lam returned the gaze. Brakan was about the same age as Chairman Kruge, with a startling shock of white hair on his head and matching sideburns that descended to his chin.

"I suppose that at least one of your objectives is to find a certain ambassador from Tsu by the name of, I believe, Altua," suggested Brakan. Lam and Lista did not confirm his guess.

"I don't blame you for mistrusting me," admitted Brakan. "But please consider what I have to say. I'm prepared to help you." Brakan watched the surprised looks on his guests' faces with delight.

"How will you help us?" asked Lam warily.

Brakan became more serious and hushed.

"I trust that you are aware of our situation on Vassir. A man who is only the Chairman of the Council of Delegates has taken over one nation completely and has an increasing control over the others. His power lust will be the ruin of our planet—it may even lead to civil war!"

Lam studied the commander's face for signs of sincerity or dishonesty, but could not read it one way or the other.

"And what would you like us to do?" he asked suspiciously.

"I will send you to Vassir by shuttle where you'll be held at the government center in the city of Wyntir in the nation of Highland. I will see that you are treated well and released as soon as possible. But while you're there, I want you to be my contact with our agent in the government center."

"Your agent?" queried Lista.

"There are many of us—in government, the army, in the market world—who are certain that Kruge is leading us to ruin. Most of us do not know each other and communicate through a complicated system of messages. There are some important and timely communications I will need to be getting and receiving from our agent at the Highland Government Center that I do not wish to trust to a series of anonymous messengers. I want you to contact him directly for me and act as my personal and direct messenger."

Lam thought it over in his mind for a moment. He looked at Lista, but she wore no expression.

"You were right earlier—we do want to find Altua," Lam said confidently, as though he actually had a choice in the matter. "Do you have any ideas where he might be?"

"No," Brakan chuckled, "but I promise you can look for the old fellow while you're in Highland."

"We also want transportation to the village of Travalia," Lam negotiated.

"It's in Woodland," Lista added.

"Very well," said Brakan, his smile a bit forced. "You are doing the solar system a great service."

Brakan rose and pressed a button on the wall as he said, "I will see that you are taken to the dining hall and given some nourishment. I'm sure you are famished." Lam's stomach painfully agreed with him. Brakan pointed to the corner at a dusty saddlebag. "And I believe that is yours—we found it near your bodies."

As Brakan spoke, the armed soldier returned and escorted Lam and Lista out of the room. Although she wore her finder, Lista held on to Lam's arm for direction.

When he was alone again, Brakan walked to a counter by a mirror on a wall and picked up the crystal jar that rested there. He pulled out the stopper and poured some of the precious liquid into one of the crystal glasses lined up along the counter. As he sipped the drink, he smiled to himself slyly.

With his drink in hand, Brakan sauntered back to his study. A dark red banner with a black hexagram and two globes covered one entire wall. He tipped his hand up in a casual salute as he entered.

Chapter Ten

If we have to be prisoners, this is the way to do it," said Lam above the electronic waves. Alone, Lam and Lista reclined on hammocks in a sophisticated environment room in the lower level of the Highland Government Center. Warm breezes poured through vents in the wall, broad-leafed trees waved above them, and the air even had a salty tang to complete the simulation of a seaside beach.

The walls of the secluded room were paneled in dark wood, and bright tile mosaics covered the floor beneath the hammocks. The two lights on walls opposite each other were tinted amber to add to the relaxing atmosphere. Soft music from strange stringed instruments drifted in from somewhere unknown. Lam did not even recognize the scale the music used. Next to his hammock, Lam had his old skip's saddlebag—he did not want it out of his sight.

They had arrived by shuttle the day before from Vassir's moon and had been treated like ambassadors ever since.

"We're not prisoners," jested Lista; "we're *guests*. Remember what Kruge told us when we arrived?"

"And that guy in the hall with the red uniform and the huge Redlyn pistol is our private bodyguard, right?"

"Lam, I think there's someone here with us," said Lista instead of laughing.

Lam opened his eyes and looked around the room, twisting to see behind them. He started when he saw a young man in a white government-center uniform.

"I'm sorry," the lad apologized. "I didn't mean to startle you."

"What do you want?" demanded Lam, somewhat annoyed at having been alarmed.

"Shh. It's very important that no one knows I am here. I know you are Lam Laeo and Lista NaWoodlander. I am Keneche Krugeson, son of Chairman Kruge of the Council of Delegates."

Lam looked shocked to hear that the young man conversing with him in Common was his adversary's son. Upon hearing the name of his visitor, he struggled to sit up straighter and gave Keneche his full attention.

"Please—it is not as sinister as you think," whispered Keneche reassuringly. "My father has many children by many wives. Those in favor hold high posts; the rest of us are government-center servants."

"What do you want?" Lam grunted.

"It is my understanding that you were rescued and captured on Elna, then sent here by Brakan, the moon-base commander."

"That's right," confirmed Lista, tilting her head as she studied the tone of Keneche's voice for signs of sincerity.

"It is also my understanding that you have been searching for a Tsuian named Altua."

"What do you know about Altua?" Lam asked.

"Did Brakan give you the impression that he was being held on Vassir, perhaps in Highland?"

"He said that we could look for him, that we were to make contact with someone who could help us."

"I am the one to help you, but please don't tell Brakan this yet. He doesn't know that I'm his contact in the Highland Government Center, and I'd like to keep it that way for now—I don't trust him."

Lam slumped back down into the hammock and looked disappointed.

"Great," he sighed. "Whom am I supposed to believe?"

"I understand your predicament," said Keneche sympathetically. "I won't tell you to believe me over a military commander. But let me propose something to you. You have probably noticed that you are more prisoner than guest here—there is no way you will be allowed the freedom to do much of anything, let alone look for a missing ambassador. If you would like to test Brakan's honesty, when he contacts you next, ask him to arrange for your escape. Lista, do you have friends in Woodland who would hide you for a while?"

"Yes," Lista said enthusiastically. "That is why I came back to Vassir."

"If Brakan can get you to Woodland, I will look for Altua. If Brakan does not help you, we know he is not on your side. If I do not find Altua in ten days, I will grant that you have no reason to trust me, either."

Lam considered his proposal. It seemed reasonable. Dangerous, but reasonable.

"I don't mean to force you into a decision, but I will have to leave quickly."

"We have a bargain," said Lam hastily. "Ten days from now, contact us at the village of Travalia in Woodland."

Keneche smiled, bowed and started across the tile to a service door in the corner.

"Wait," said Lam, struggling to get up from his hammock. "I'm crazy to give you this," Lam continued, "but it may help you find Altua." He reached into his saddlebag and pulled out the M-stone amulet Padu had given him. Keneche took it and looked puzzled. "When the stone glows brighter, you'll know you're getting closer to Altua."

Keneche pocketed the blue amulet and hurried to the service door. He pulled a small card from his pocket and held it to a gold button near the door's handle. It slid open and Keneche slipped through. Almost simultaneously, the main door opened and a Redlyn pistol, followed by Lam and Lista's "bodyguard," leaned in. The guard's stern gaze revealed nothing. He nodded an apology for the intrusion and ducked out again.

"This is getting complicated," said Lista, reaching for the cool fruit drink beneath her.

"I wonder if Hud knew it would be like this?"

"Who?"

"Never mind. I'm sure he did."

Lam opened his eyes and saw Elna's light spilling through the leaded glass panes of his window. But he did not look to see what woke him up. He scratched his nose and closed his eyes again, but this time felt the tapping on his shoulder. He rolled over in his bed, then nearly jumped out the other side when he saw the intruder.

There was a tall figure dressed in black leather. Highly burnished black armor covered his shoulders, chest and groin. A black helmet with a reflective visor covering his eyes protected his head. A shoulder blaster hung from his back by a black canvas strap.

"I'm from Brakan," a deep voice explained to the startled sleeper. The sight of the armored warrior and the name of "Brakan" jolted him out of any lingering drowsiness. He quickly recalled that Brakan had contacted him only a day before, and Lam had done as Keneche suggested—he asked that Brakan arrange for their release.

"How do I know you're from Brakan?" Lam questioned the intruder. The warrior said nothing but threw a small object onto Lam's bed. Lam picked it up with reservation, but quickly identified it as his own Redlyn pistol. Next, a stack of clothes hurled toward him and landed in his lap. They were black and, as was the custom with Highland clothes, lined with animal fur.

"Put them on," Lam's frightening benefactor ordered.

"What's going on?" asked Lam while he obediently pulled on the tunic and trousers.

"You are leaving Highland tonight."

"Why the middle of the night?"

"Did you think that Kruge would open the doors and let you out like a house pet?" taunted his benefactor.

Lam chose not to answer that, but realized that Brakan was having to go to extreme measures to secure his freedom.

"Brakan needs to know where he can contact you," said the black figure as Lam struggled to pull his boots over the trousers.

"I'm not sure I should say," grunted Lam. In response, the armored giant swung the blaster from his shoulder and snapped the activator. He did not aim it directly at Lam, but the seriousness of his intentions struck Lam like a chain mail glove.

"Travalia in Woodland," Lam sputtered hastily.

Lam's rescuer relaxed a little, to Lam's relief, but as soon as

Lam had pulled on his last boot, the black-gloved hand motioned him to the partially open door.

"Where's Lista?"

"Waiting."

On his way to the door, he passed his dressing stand. Lam reached into his wrecked skip's saddlebag, grabbed the Le-in stone, and pocketed it.

"What?" exclaimed Lam in a loud whisper as he opened the door and found he had to step over the fallen body of his guard. The red uniformed man lay face-down in a red pool.

We're not playing games here, he told himself. He spotted Lista leaning against one of the red and black hexagram banners. She heard him come and whispered his name.

"Yes, it's me," Lam assured her.

"Move quickly!" The black helmet and lowered visor distorted his voice and made his order sound menacing. Lam grabbed Lista's hand and they hurried down the hall, led by the commando. Lam's heart raced as they rushed secretly down the empty halls. He had his own Redlyn pistol readied at each corner and open door, ready to incinerate anyone who discovered them but desperately hoping he would not have to.

"In here!" their rescuer whispered harshly as he pointed with his blaster into a darkened room. Lam went first and led Lista in by the hand, although Lista with her finder would have done a better job navigating the oppressively dark room. Lam could tell by the chemical smells that they were in a utility room.

"To the end," they heard the authoritative voice order. Lam finally saw the end he was looking for. Dim light crept into the room through an open window at the far wall. Lam spun around when he heard footsteps behind him.

"Keep going! They are just searching the hallway."

Lam obeyed and rushed to the window. Looking out he saw a small ship similar to the kind he used to fly for fun on Entar. It was on a flat section of the roof a few precarious steps from the window. The hatch was open on top like a lid and Lam could see that there was only room for two and that it was empty.

"How are you getting out of here?" Lam asked their rescuer.

"If you were from our planet, you wouldn't ask a Valorian such a question."

"Be careful, Lista," Lam warned as he threw one leg over the sill. "The roof is pitched here. Lie on your stomach and crawl sideways. I'll be waiting for you on the flat section and help you into the ship."

Lam lowered himself to the wood shake roof and watched to make sure Lista was coming. She deftly swung out and landed beside him, but as she did, he saw light emerge from the hallway door. The room crackled brilliantly as Redlyn bolts hurled from hostile weapons and shattered woodwork.

"That guy'll hold them off for a while," Lam comforted Lista as they crept to the ship. A couple of red bolts of energy pierced the wall and sang above their heads. Lam urged his limbs to move as fast as he dared. It was only moments, but it seemed longer, and Lam dropped to the level roof. He called Lista to make sure she knew where to jump, and she followed Lam's lead to the roof and he steadied her as she landed.

Lam inhaled a breath of relief but nearly choked on it when he looked down and saw soldiers streaming into the courtyard from the government-center building beneath them. A few soldiers quickly spotted the ship on the roof and called to each other while others aimed their shoulder blasters.

"Come on!" called Lam, pulling Lista toward the ship. He guided Lista's foot to the running board and boosted her into the cockpit. Lam jumped onto the running board, leaned back and discharged a few blasts from his pistol into the small army below.

"Just to keep you busy!" he called as he fired a final volley and heaved himself awkwardly into the ship. The soldiers ceased fire for a moment to scramble for cover from Lam's wild shooting.

As the clear hatch hissed closed over them, Lam panicked for a moment when he saw the seemingly unfamiliar controls. Then he ignored the stylistic differences and grabbed the control column as he pressed the instigation panel. A low hum instantly filled the ship and Lam stole one last glimpse over the roof to make sure his path was clear. It wasn't.

Redlyn bolts pierced the night sky all around the ship. The red glow lit up Lam's face as he gritted his teeth. He pulled back on the controls and felt the g-forces slam him against his seat as they shot into flight. Fighting the urge to close his eyes, Lam watched the attack they hoped to be escaping in a moment.

The ship lurched and Lista held her ears as a loud tearing sound filled the cockpit. "What was that?" she asked fearfully.

"We've been hit," said Lam. By the time he told her, they were already too high for the soldiers below to see, and too far away for them to be accurate. Lam scanned the instruments, written in Highland Vassirian, and announced to Lista, "As near as I can tell, we didn't sustain any terminal damage."

"Good. Then we can put plenty of distance between us and those trigger-happy troops back there."

"Oh, we'll get far enough away from them all right, but it seemed too easy."

"Perhaps the Power protected us."

"Perhaps," replied Lam. "I have to admit that the Power is all that has kept me alive up until now. The 'coincidence' of being discovered near death on the dark side of Elna is a good example of that. But this seemed different—they were all there, saw us clearly, but hesitated shooting. Then when they did, they missed."

"I wouldn't complain," said Lista, reaching over and punching Lam lightly on the arm.

In the government-center courtyard, Highland soldiers dangled their weapons as they waited for them to cool enough to sling them back over their shoulders.

"You fool!" yelled the squad leader to one of the troops. "How could you shoot so poorly?"

"I'm sorry, sir. I didn't mean to hit him, but I wanted to make it look like I tried."

"Thank the gods that he got away," said the squad leader, shaking his head. "I won't recommend your termination this time, but spend more time at the range!"

In the utility room, the black-armored commando looked out the shattered window and saw that Lam's borrowed ship was well out of range.

"He's gone," he called into the hall. The shooting stopped and the commando strolled into the hall. Lam and Lista's former guard, covered with red stains that looked like blood, was waiting with the other soldiers in the hall.

"I hope this stuff comes off my skin," he complained, rubbing the excess from his face.

"The cook said it would," said the black-armored commando, removing his helmet to reveal a sweaty bush of white hair.

"Good performance, Brakan," the first commended, reaching up to slap the older man on the back. "You looked just like a Valorian."

"That was the plan, Kaman," Brakan muttered.

"I know you don't think much of the Valorians, but our plan worked!" Kaman said cheerfully.

"So far," Brakan admitted, mustering a little better show of enthusiasm. "But don't be so confident. Remember the proverb, 'A light heart loses wars.' "

"You'd better get used to my style," Kaman warned through a belligerent smile.

Chapter Eleven

What do you mean we can't land?" exclaimed Lista in a panic. Their craft hurled through the air above the treetops of Woodland like an arrow searching for its mark.

"I mean that wild shot back at the government center demolished the long cycle melder on this thing's gravity resistor." Lam's retort revealed his aggravation. "We either have to cruise until we drop for lack of fuel, or we crash land."

"Maybe we could land at Port Cloud in Woodland—they must have emergency help."

"Sure. And what do we tell them when they ask the name of our craft, our destination, identification, our origin, our authorization?"

"Do you have a better solution?" Lista asked.

"Just keep directing us to Travalia."

Lam was relieved that Lista's descriptions seemed to match his aeriel perspective. He swung the sleek craft onto a course above the road that led to the crip village from the aeriel port of Woodland. Woodland was not populated or wealthy enough for a spaceport, but the smaller craft that used the facility were a vital link to the rest of Vassir. Food, textiles and other exports flew out of Woodland's port in exchange for goods Woodland could not produce.

"Now follow the river north, did you say?" Lam asked.

"North," Lista said. "Much of the work done by the Travalians is shipped by water to Port Cloud. The Snowy River actually can be traveled all the way to Highland."

Lam was almost glad that Lista could not see the landscape careening beneath them. He hugged the treetops and terrain as closely as he could to avoid detection by tracking devices. This was the only precaution he could take, however—if Highland sent planes after him, nothing would help.

"Speaking of rivers," said Lam dryly, "can you swim?"

"Not very well."

"Then a water landing is out."

The horizon had turned from dark black to gray since they began their flight, and Lam realized that dawn would be breaking soon.

"At least I will be able to see what we are crashing into," said Lam. "It is starting to get light."

"Listen here, Mr. Doom," demanded Lista. "There is a long stretch of road leading into town that will be vacant this time of morning. I know it'll be tough on the paint job, but it should work as an emergency landing strip."

Lam was embarrassed. He was used to being the one to save the day.

"I think I see it," Lam confirmed flatly.

Travalia was larger than Lam had expected. Hundreds of large and small buildings clustered together on the level acres among the hills. The entire village, Lam could see from above, was surrounded by woods and thick vegetation. The river cut it neatly in two, and seemed to be the center of activity.

Lam circled the road that would serve as a landing strip once, getting his bearings and his nerve.

"This will get them up bright and early," said Lam as he checked his shoulder strap. "Make sure you are secure in your seat, but I'd keep one hand on your strap release—we may have to make a quick getaway."

Right after the last bend in the road before the village, Lam eased their small ship down. The landing pads that usually descended during landing would just dig into the dirt road and flip them over, Lam decided. This landing would be a belly-burner.

"Hang on," warned Lam as the road rose up to meet the falling craft.

A grinding noise screamed through the cockpit and Lam had all he could do to keep from letting go of the controls to cover his ears as Lista was doing. Lam felt as if the vibrations would shake the ship and the riders into component parts as they skidded along the gravel.

Lam strained at the controls, trying to keep on the road. His eyes widdened with horror as he felt their tail begin to swing to the right. Lam tried to compensate, but only managed to swing the tail in the other direction. Each attempt to straighten it threw them more out of control. There was nothing more he could do. The tail fought him and skidded to the side, and then all the way around, spinning the ship in circles.

There was no way to control it now, and Lam simply held on to avoid rattling like a seed in a dry pod. The careening craft was on its third revolution, heading for the woods, when the tail hit the brush. The scrub snapped harmlessly out of the way, and even slowed the ship down some, but not enough to prevent it from colliding with a stout fir tree. The tail cracked against the tree and the ship lurched to a stop. The ground smoldered from the friction, and the propellant dripped down the cracked and overheated fuselage. A small fire was already burning beneath the swept-back left wing.

In the cockpit, the heads of both passengers hung down, their limp bodies held up only by their safety straps.

Lassen's wife was waiting for him at the door of his dwelling at the compound that night. He dropped his satchel when he saw her and gathered her into his arms and did not let her go. She finally pushed him gently back and studied his face in the subdued hallway light.

"Normally I'd welcome a greeting like that," she said softly. "But I can see there's something wrong." She knew Lassen had been troubled since the problems with the Council started. But this was different—this was not a perplexed or thoughtful look; it was a sad and determined look.

"There's going to be war," Lassen told her as gently as he could. She closed her eyes and let the news sink in. They had been through it years ago against the Dominion, and recollections of the preparation, the turmoil, the fear, and the grief flooded over her.

Lassen walked with her to the ornately carved wooden

bench in the greeting room of their home. She sat down, put her face in her hands and wept softly. Lassen put his arm around her and sat in silence. He could think of nothing to say that sounded appropriate.

"I guess I knew it would happen," she said tearfully. "But I always prayed to the gods that it would not." Lassen's wife glanced over and frowned at the idol there. Votive candles illumined the carved wooden face and the stains where drink offerings had been poured over its head.

"It has ears, but it can't hear my plea, can it?"

Lassen smiled sympathetically. "No."

Lassen's wife sighed and leaned back on the couch.

"When will it begin, and who will fight with us?" she asked, accepting the conflict's reality.

"We plan to begin deployment in ten days. We'll be marching with Seaward and Sundor, and we'll join forces with the Woodland militia in northwestern Woodland. From there we'll launch our attack on Highland. We're having to use mostly ancient foot-fighting strategy because Highland controls all the advanced weaponry built under Kruge's rearming. He can shoot down orbiting fighters from any of his defense satellites, and his air fleet is far superior to ours. But we believe that if we can engage them on their territory, they will be unable to use their most destructive weapons, and we will be able to out-fight them because of our advantage in numbers."

Lassen's wife nodded her understanding, and then fell into Lassen's arms.

"I'm so scared," she said almost inaudibly.

"I know," he said simply, but wanting to say much more. Ten days to say all the things he wanted to tell her. Ten days to make sure all the younger children knew that he loved them, and that the older children understood their responsibility in case . . .

Night was Jobee's friend. The teenager from Travalia liked the quiet and the stars and the crispness in the air. Nighttime was also when the River Rainers were the hungriest, and there was nothing Jobee liked better than to trap the delicious little water creatures. That night he had a whole basket full—plenty to feast on himself and sell at the Travalia dock market on the Snowy River.

Jobee yawned and shifted the basket to his other shoulder as he walked the road back to the village. He was looking forward to getting home—the friends in his house would be waking soon and it would be time for breakfast. Good thing, too, because as usual he ate all the food he packed right away. He always regretted that, but could never remember to spread his munching over the entire night.

It was about that time that he first heard it—the screaming in the air that seemed to be getting closer. Jobee stopped and scanned the sky for the source of the noise. He raised his hand above his thick brow to shield his eyes from the still-unseen sun.

"Oh, no, it's headed right for us!" he said thickly to the River Rainers in his basket. He scrambled for the woods by the side of the road, but the craft that seemed to be attacking came too fast for him to reach cover, so he just dropped down into the shallow drainage ditch and covered his head.

He pried open his eyes just long enough to see the dust cloud billow from behind the craft as it skidded on the gravel, sending sparks and loose stones flying from beneath it. The forest floor shook when it collided with the tree and began to burn.

As soon as Jobee was sure nothing else was falling from the sky, he pushed aside his basket and crawled up to the road. Through the shattered hatch he saw two bodies, and he ran toward the wreckage, calling, "Are you all right?"

Jobee pulled frantically at the clear fragments of the hatch. "I think they're alive," he assured himself. His thick lips pressed together as he concentrated his size and brawn on his work. He tugged at the safety straps but they wouldn't budge. Taking a moment for his slow mind to think, he reached down to his boot and pulled out his fishing knife. The straps yielded easily to the sharp instrument. He was on the pilot's side, so standing on the crumpled wing, he heaved out Lam's limp frame and carried him to the ditch opposite the road.

Jobee hurried back to the craft and worked to free the woman. He scraped his arm on the jagged hatch fragments, but managed to pull Lista out of the cockpit. She was lighter, and he ran across the road, holding her as he felt the heat of the burning craft behind him. As he laid her gently down, a glimmer of recognition crossed his face.

"L-Lista?" he said in amazement. "Please be all right!" he pleaded with her unconscious form when he realized who it was. "I wish someone would come and tell me you will be all right."

A loud hissing sound from the burning ship stole away his attention from his old friend. With a yell of panic, he fell over his charges, shielding them as much as he could.

A tremendous explosion rocked the woods. Pieces of metal sang above their heads, the sound of it echoing through the countryside. After that Jobee heard ringing, but couldn't tell if it was the village bell ringing or the ringing in his ears. When he dared look up, he saw a growing crowd from the village rushing to the crash site with buckets to bring water up from the river—it would take a while for the hoses to be connected to the pumps, so this older method would have to be used for the immediate crisis. The dry grass and leaves on the forest floor crackled and threatened to ignite into a forest fire.

"Over here! Over here!" shouted Jobee, jumping up and down and waving his arms. "It's Lista!"

The room was very quiet and peaceful except for a low hum. *Strange*, Lista thought. *It has not been quiet or peaceful for a long time.* She found that her eyelids resisted opening as if they had forgotten that she was blind and would not be disturbed by the light.

Beside her bed in the homey room was an elderly man with long white hair tied back from his face—it was the only way to tame the mop that had long ago grown wild. He sat in a chair that floated above the ground, held up by a small gravity resistor—the source of the droning hum. His kind blue eyes looked upon Lista's bandaged frame from a beardless face creased by the weight of difficult years. The lines of his face were drawn by years of concern, but not worry, laughter, but not levity.

"My dear Lista," he spoke gently as he saw her awaken. "Why couldn't you simply coast up quietly in a skip?"

"Aba?" she called out in a reverent whisper. She reached her hand out and felt his hand reaching for hers. She worked her way to the edge of the couch and flung her arms around him, tears flowing freely from her eyes. She was overwhelmed by her emotions—she had not expected them to be so strong. How much she missed her home and the man that the residents of Travalia called "Aba"! Feeling his loving arms around her made the world somehow manageable again.

"I feel like you slipped me some of the restorative pain reliever Travalia is so famous for," Lista laughed.

"Good morning, Lista," a familiar voice called to her from the door. It was actually afternoon, but Lam thought the greeting was appropriate since she had just regained consciousness. He had already changed out of his Highland clothes into a more appropriate Woodland costume.

"Is that the Prince of the Perfect Landings?" asked Lista.

"If you're going to complain about getting roughed up a little, wait until you hear what happened to the ship," Lam continued good-naturedly.

The three laughed together as Lam helped Lista sit upright on the couch, and then joined her. "I know you and Lista probably have much to talk about," Lam told the venerable leader of Travalia. "Lista has told me about your village, but I had no idea it was so large and industrious."

"Then you have had a chance to visit a little? To take a little tour?" asked the proud patriarch of the village.

"And to meet some of the people here," added Lam. "I noticed that not everyone is ill."

"Many of the children who are born here stay," Aba explained so Lam wouldn't have to continue stumbling for understanding. "And others come from as far away as Seaward to help us—to spend their lives working here in exchange for food, a place to live, and a lot of love."

"So tell me," urged Lista eagerly, "what has happened since I've been gone?"

Aba hung his gray head for a moment. The laugh lines gave way to lines of concern and he began to explain.

"I wish I had good news for you," Aba answered earnestly.

"But I know I could not hide it from you, anyway—you have always had a way of perceiving when things were not right."

Aba looked at Lam as he spoke since Lista could not see him. "We received a sealed message from the Council of Delegates. It was signed by the ministry of restoration and said that we were to be inspected for certain 'health violations' believed to exist here."

"What does that mean?" asked Lista flatly, her face already losing color.

"We have heard rumors of distressing activities in the Highland Resoration Seminary," said Aba with pained difficulty. "The sick, if they are weak or old, are reportedly treated with a 'low-energy diet.' Friends, we have reason to believe they are being starved to death."

After a pause to let his words sink in, Aba continued.

"Lista, do you remember a boy named Gadeen? No? It doesn't matter who he is really, except that his mother had little control over her legs and his father was born with short and malformed arms. They met in Travalia—outcasts from the rest of Vassir, as almost all of us are. They married and had a normal son, Gadeen." Aba paused to make sure his listeners followed him.

"Gadeen was forced to join the Highland militia a little over a year ago and was assigned to the Restoration Seminary. It is a common assignment for a new soldier—an undesirable one because they have to guard the annex that houses the insane."

Aba was a good storyteller, but Lam and Lista couldn't help being anxious for him to reach the point of the tale.

"One night," continued Aba, "he had to help carry out and bury the dead body of one of the annex inmates. Gadeen didn't think much of it until the next night when he had to bury two more. He discreetly asked some of his comrades about it, and they told him the inmates were being 'treated' and 'processed.' They also told him similar stories about criminals in prison. Well, Gadeen asked for a transfer and they sent him to the government center—to keep an eye on him, I think. This is in the strictest confidence now—he told me when he was here visiting a short time ago that he was involved in some sort of countermovement that opposes Chairman Kruge."

A shudder ran through Lista as she and Lam sat in stunned silence. Finally Lam spoke.

"There is not much room on the new Vassir, is there? What do you think they'll do when they come here?"

Aba shook his head in near-despair. "We fear the worst."

"When are they scheduled to come?" asked Lam, his mind beginning to review the possible options the village had. It was flee or fight as far as he could see it. Both choices sounded bleak.

"I am afraid we have only ten days."

Chapter Twelve

Lam stood in the shade of the tent with Lista and listened as a woman explained her craft of weaving. The tent was one of many brightly colored booths set up on the wooden dock banking the Snowy River that curved through the village of Travalia. She was an older woman, not very attractive, but friendly and enthusiastic as she demonstrated her loom.

Lam watched the shuttle fly through what looked to him like a bewildering maze of colored threads. Almost miraculously the cloth took shape before his eyes. Lista had told Lam the woman's story, so he knew how her head was injured in a fall as a child and how she was later abandoned when her parents realized that she would never fully recover. Lam knew she could probably not read or write, but her well-practiced craft came naturally to her now, and fine cloth with bright patterns blossomed out of her loom.

Her work was so fine, as were many of the crafts there, that buyers and merchants from Highland to Sundor traveled the Snowy River for wares to resell to government officials, Council delegates and other wealthy men and women. Lam's anger grew hotter. *I can see Kruge now, with a tablecloth made by this woman,* he thought, *spreading a feast for his fat friends with the rare mushrooms so meticulously nurtured and cultivated in woods by the Travalians — and then endorsing an "inspection" that will lead to many of the villagers "vanishing" like the criminals and insane seem to have been doing.*

"You do beautiful work," Lam told the woman, returning to the present. "Thank you for taking the time to show me how you do this."

"I like to show you," the simple woman said with delight.

"Come again, come again soon—I show you more."

Lam's tension would not let his feet stay in one place long, so he thanked her again and led Lista back to the boardwalk. He had hoped to hear from Keneche about Altua long before this.

"What do you think?" asked Lista as they strolled the sunny street. They had been there several days, and Lam had seen many of the artisans at work. They strolled past the shops and booths that lined the river where the industrious craftsmen and women cobbled, smithed, sewed, cooked, and otherwise worked to support themselves and others in the village who could not work.

"I'm astonished," admitted Lam. "These are hardly the worthless people Kruge talked about in his speech."

"I don't think he even knows what goes on here—everyone contributes. Even those who are too sick to get up give us the gift of caring—they bring out the best in us, the selflessness. The thing Kruge and his kind forget is that no one is perfect. Who's to say how healthy someone must be to live?"

"When I first met the Friend, it was in a dream—a very realistic dream," said Lam thoughtfully.

"I know the kind you mean," Lista interjected. "The kind where you can sense your surroundings."

"Exactly. I could feel the burning heat of the desert. My throat burned from the dryness and I was certain that I would soon perish in the wasteland. The next thing I knew, a very strange man helped me to the safety of a cave. His appearance was weatherworn—it looked as if he had suffered years of cruel desert living. When he spoke to me, his words ripped open my heart, but at the same time healed it—like when you scrape your skin and wash it clean until it hurts, then put a healing balm on it.

"When I see your friends, I think of the Friend and how he suffers with us in all our pain, all our deformities, all our grief."

Lista listened to Lam share more personally than he ever had with her, and it touched her. She wanted him to continue so that she could feel more a part of him, and learn more about the One he served so recklessly.

"Why does he do it?" Lista asked as they paused at a tent

where a woman peddled beautiful flowers she and her house-mates had grown.

"Suffer with us?" Lam asked. "We all have the same Source, and the Power gives us all life." Lam picked up a ceramic vase that held a spray of exotic blooms. Long tapering stems ended in fur-like balls that looked like starbursts as dozens of lavender threads jutted out from a cone and ended in yellow points. "In a way we are like these flowers. He created them each beauti-fully, and each reflects his beauty. He created each of us to be like him, and no matter how battered and broken we are, we still reflect his beauty."

Lista remained thoughtful for a moment as she brushed her fingers along the flowers' delicate petals and drank in their sweet fragrance.

"Somehow that all makes sense," she said quietly. "Even if people like Kruge don't see it, I know there is beauty in each of these people. Maybe not being able to see their physical ap-pearance helps me understand that."

"I don't think so," Lam said. "You just know what is im-portant and what isn't. It isn't important what people can do, what they look like, how smart they are—it's just that they *are*."

Lam's story sparked her own desire for hope. She wished she could lose herself in faith in the Friend, but she was afraid to hope—she'd been let down too many times.

"Why did you never tell me all this before?" Lista asked with a playful sternness.

"I don't like to talk about myself."

"I certainly can't accuse you of spending too much time reminiscing," Lista agreed.

"I guess another reason I haven't talked about it is that I needed to be reminded of it myself."

Lam put down the vase, took Lista's hand and they contin-ued up the market. There happened to be quite a few visitors there that morning, and a few boys skipped around a square outlined with brightly painted sticks while others played a Woodland folksong on their pipes. On occasion, a market-goer would toss a coin into the square and the boys would jump a little higher in their dance.

"That's a good saying—'it's just that they are,' " said Lista as they stood and listened to the cheerful music. "It's not this way in Woodland, but in Highland the tradition is not to even discuss a baby's name until he is safely delivered. I guess that way they don't feel any guilt when the baby 'vanishes' like the prisoners we heard about. The practice is quite common there. But even the Restoration Seminary in Highland where I studied teaches that nothing unusual happens to the baby when it is born. Only a few days after new life is conceived, his tiny heart begins to beat," said Lista in awe. "One time not too long ago, a baby came to our village—left here in a box of rags. Her tiny body was bruised, and it was clear to us that her mother had tried to make her 'vanish,' but when she saw that what she was attempting to get rid of was really a tiny life, she probably felt guilty enough to leave her here.

"It was too late for us to do anything to save her—she was so tiny, she probably couldn't have lived anyway, but we loved her, fed her as best we could, and tried to make her comfortable. She was so weak she didn't even cry. The night before she died, I held her cradled in my arms while Aba read to us. I heard him stop reading for a moment. 'Why, Lista,' he said softly, 'I could swear the child just smiled at you.' "

Lam could tell it was an emotional story for Lista. He put his arm around her while she paused.

The tenderness he felt for Lista at that moment, the love he was developing for the Travalians, even his unfinished search for Altua clashed with his mental image of Kruge—cold, cruel, oblivious to the beauty in Travalia.

"My fault is my sightlessness," Lista continued about the baby; "hers was her age. But I believe you are right; we have the same Source and are important just because we *are*."

"You're more than important," Lam said as he pulled her a little closer. "You're priceless."

Lista smiled shyly and put one hand to her cheek to see if she was as flushed as she suddenly suspected.

"Forget it, Krugeson," said a brash young man dressed in the Highland Government Center guard uniform. He was not a soldier, but was relegated to guard duty near the underground skip port for several hours each night. He sat in a small room surrounded by shelves full of security paraphernalia. There were a few Redlyn pistols and riot helmets, but most of the shelves held name badges and electronic keys to the government-center rooms and vehicles.

"What do you mean 'forget it'?" Keneche persisted.

"I mean they'd feed me to the Bashamptas if they found out I gave you a master key."

"And what do you think they would have done if I hadn't captured that vagrant who tried to steal the Chairman's skip—the vagrant who walked right past you while you were sleeping off the celebration you had at your post—who walked right through the door you left unlocked because you were too drunk to put the key in the lock."

"I guess I do owe you one," admitted the guard grudgingly.

"You sure do. So can you help me?"

The guard rubbed his chin in pained concentration.

"The hospitality minister will be traveling to the agriculture market in north Highland to pick up supplies for some big up-pity-up party they're having. He'll be checking in his key while he's gone, so I suppose you could use it for a few hours while I'm on duty that evening—if you *swear* to get it back before my relief comes."

"By the gods," Keneche promised. "When will this be?"

"Seven days from today."

"What?" gasped Keneche. "That is the last possible moment it will be of use to me—I can't wait that long!"

"Sorry, Krugeson. You'll have to. You can tell them about the vagrant if you want to; I still can't get you anything before then."

Keneche had to agree to the terms, although he had to rub his neck to keep it from tangling itself in a tension knot while they arranged the details.

*I'll have to find out **exactly** where Altua is before then,* Keneche told himself as he climbed the little-used and ill-lit stairs from the skip port. *And I'll have to get to Lam immediately. The ten days will be up by then, and Lam may spill everything to Brakan if I don't* *get to him with Altua by then, and I'm not at all sure that old moon crater Brakan can be trusted.*

Lam tossed a stone into the slowly moving water, and the current carried the ripples gently downstream. He had managed to get away from Lista and Aba, and the crowd that usually hung around asking where he came from.

Lista warned him about going out at dusk without snapper syrup, but he didn't care. She said that if the night snappers come out of the ground, he'd have to throw them some sweet syrup or they'd come after *him*. He hadn't seen one of the little predators yet. His solitude only sharpened the feeling of help-lessness that gnawed at him more deeply each day. The sun was well past the horizon, and the fading colors had all but relin-quished the sky to the descending deep blue of night. Lam's mood matched the night better than the sunset, anyway.

He plucked a tall piece of grass from the bank beside him, set it between his teeth and lay back to watch the stars slowly emerge. The smooth flat stone that rippled the river reminded him of one just like it in his pocket. Lam reached into the pocket of his tunic and felt the hard gift from the Le-in. He pulled it out and examined it in the fading light. "A three-cornered leaf, one corner each for the Source, the Power, and the Friend," Lam said, recalling the explanation the Le-in gave him. "And carved in stone, a symbol of strength and eternity."

"Oaak," called a night-feeding bird that fluttered to a land-ing on the branch above Lam's head. It craned its neck out and examined Lam with its large yellow eyes.

"Couldn't sleep either?" Lam asked the bird. It blinked slowly as it regarded him intently. "I'll give you some advice—pack up and move out of this town as soon as you can. There's big trouble coming."

"Oaak," the bird replied knowingly.

"I wouldn't blame you one bit. As a matter of fact, the thought crossed my mind that I'd be smart to do the same, but I couldn't do that. I guess the thing that kills me is that there's nothing I can do. Before, there was always a way to fight back, but this time it would be a little tough. What am I supposed to do, scrounge up a few guns and grenades—maybe a fighter or two, and train the Travalians into an army that can stand up against the new equipment Kruge has? Am I supposed to go to Kruge and persuade him not to interfere? Ha! How about if I assassinate him? Now that would be a trick, wouldn't it?"

Lam's feathered confidant craned its neck and tipped its head to one side as if it were really trying to understand what he said.

"I could topple a superpower that had conquered most of the civilized galaxy, but I can't protect a few poor people from one crazy man."

"Oaak!" exclaimed the bird loudly.

"You're right. It wasn't me that toppled the Dominion—it was the Source." Lam looked past his curious companion and up to the stars.

"Friend," he said softly, with pain and frustration evident in his voice, "there are so many people who worship stones or pieces of wood; there are so many people in this galaxy who are possessed by their own greed and selfishness. You freed me from that, but lately I've been acting as though everything depends on me—and not bothering to find out what you want."

Lam sighed as he poured out his confession—it drained him, but drained him of feelings he didn't care for anyway.

"I'm frightened. In three days, the inspectors will be here. How many people here will qualify as 'health violations'? If Lista and I are found, we'll probably be taken prisoner—probably killed. But I can't leave these people here to face Kruge's goons by themselves."

Lam closed his eyes as they began to sting. His throat began to constrict and he knew his emotions were beginning to overwhelm him. For once, he didn't care. He was desperate, afraid, but at least not alone—in his mind he pictured himself sitting on the riverbank next to the Friend. His warmth and power seemed to radiate to Lam, giving him strength. Without expecting it, a strong conviction developed in Lam—a course of action that seemed to make so much sense he wondered why he hadn't thought of it earlier.

"That's what I'll do," Lam told his yellow-eyed audience.

"Maybe I was so anxious, I couldn't believe it would help."

Lam quickly sat up and startled the bird, which took flight. He put the stone in his pocket, rose stiffly to his feet and struck back to Travalia, determined and inspired.

Kruge ran his hand across the control panel of his ship as though he were caressing a woman. He could smell the newness of it, and feel its power even though the only systems activated at the moment were the interior lights, and those only dimly.

It was the flagship of the gray-haired Chairman's fleet, built during the rearming for the defense of Vassir. He smiled to himself as he considered how closely the defense needs paralleled his own needs. This was much better than when he was governor under the Dominion—now he was the recipient of the wealth, and the final authority. There were only a few trouble spots, and he intended to dispose of those shortly.

"Father?" he heard a voice call from near the ship's hatch.

"Is that the Minister of Energy Resources and Commander of the Ground Militia?" Kruge answered. Kaman laughed and stepped into the ship; he pressed a panel, and the hatch hissed closed.

"Do you have news for me?" asked Kruge, motioning for his son to be seated in the navigator's seat while he sat in the communications seat and swiveled his chair to face him.

"In two days the dissident armies will begin their march."

"Good," Kruge grinned widely. "Is everything ready for them?"

"Yes, Father. It should be a historic day. The entire militia is assembled. When the day comes, we'll be ready for them with armed skips and transports, ener-bolt throwers and new hand-held weapons for the troops—all compliments of the rearming. We expect the other armies to have no weapons newer than 15 years old, no heavy guns or armed vehicles."

"Lassen will regret the day he turned on the new Vassir," Kruge hissed. "I, of course, will keep a small contingent of guards here to protect the government center. The Valorians will also be here under my personal command for me to dispatch if need be."

"Of course," Kaman answered hastily. "The regular forces and the Valorians are not the best comrades anyway. The militia is jealous, and some people think the Valorians' allegiance to Highland is tenuous."

"Brakan is their chief critic," Kruge said. "But I know our Highland Valorians are loyal to me. Other countries may have trouble with their Valorians, but ours are more loyal than Brakan."

"About Brakan—" Kaman started.

"I know Brakan doesn't have complete faith in your ability to lead the army. Leave him to me. I have faith in you, and after this victory, the people will love you as they do me. When I die, you will serve well as the solar system's ruler."

"I'm not concerned about that old bag of moon dust," Kaman assured. "I just wanted to tell you that our plan to find our security leak is going well."

"What is the fool's name who is helping us unknowingly?"

"Lam Laeo, and his companion, some crip woman."

"Tell Brakan not to get overconfident with this Laeo. I heard he had something to do with the fall of the Dominion. I wish I didn't have to depend on Brakan."

"He likes me giving him orders about as much as a River Rainer likes boiling water, but I'll tell him. Anything else?"

"Tell your mother I will see her tonight—I wish to celebrate," he said, leaning back in his seat. Well-laid plans always pleased him, and he intended to make sure these plans succeeded.

Chapter Thirteen

Lam has a visitor," a girl who was sweeping Aba's porch called into the house.

Lam had been having lunch with Lista and Aba, but had not been able to eat much anyway. He hastily excused himself and rushed out to the porch to meet his caller.

"Lam Laeo? I am from Brakan," said the young officer. He was dressed in ordinary Highland clothes, but wore a pentagram badge on his left arm with three bars above it indicating his rank in the military. "Where can we talk?"

Lam motioned to a chair on the porch, and the officer looked as though he might protest for a more private site, then decided it would do. Lam sat next to him and looked to the road and the woods. It had rained that morning, and now that the sun was out, the evaporating water cast a haze over the landscape, making it look like a painting.

"Brakan would like to meet you tomorrow night," said the messenger, not wasting any time.

"I want to see him today," Lam replied firmly.

The officer scowled at this unexpected complication.

"That is not possible," the officer replied, his gray eyes revealing a hint of uncertainty.

"You don't understand," Lam insisted. "We have only a few days before it will be too late—I must see him today."

The messenger began to look a little ruffled and retorted, "I happen to know that he is engaged this evening."

"Do you happen to know if he is engaged tomorrow at dawn?" Lam pushed.

"No, I don't know," the officer finally admitted.

"Then tell him I will meet him tomorrow at dawn."

"I'll tell him, but I can't promise he will be there."

"Tell him I'll be there at dawn, and if he is not, I'll leave and will give him no information."

"Where shall he meet you?" asked the officer, growing quite annoyed with Lam's demands.

"In Port Cloud's public park on the Snowy River." Lam recited his planned directions.

The officer nodded and rose to leave. Lam watched him walk to the road and swing his leg onto his one-man skip. He slipped a helmet over his head and lowered the visor as the skip hummed to life. In a swift movement he pushed the skip forward, banked it, and sped away.

"Tomorrow is the tenth day for Keneche, and his time will be up," Lam mused. "Kruge's henchmen are due in just a few days, and Brakan is the only one I know who might be able to help." He looked to the sky and sighed, "Friend, that's cutting it awfully close—I hope you know what you are doing."

The bolt erupted from Lassen's shoulder blaster and hurled harmlessly past the silhouetted figure of a man in the distance. Lassen, on his stomach in the grass, quickly fired again, this time carving off a piece of the figure's shoulder.

"Not bad," said the practice range leader, squinting at the only slightly damaged wooden target. "But I would leave the actual shooting to us."

"Thanks for the confidence," chided Lassen as he stood and handed the powerful weapon back to the range leader.

Lassen took a moment to watch the whirlwind of activity in the military camp outside his mining town in Redland. The rhythmic sounds of footfalls on the road echoed off the hills as squads of black-armored soldiers ran in drill formation. The air crackled with blaster bolts from practicing marksmen. Squad commanders barked orders to heavy-laden troops who loaded bundled supplies, weapons, and spare parts onto transports in preparation for the long overland march.

"Ho there, Husband Lassen," hailed Lassen's wife as she brought her skip delicately to a halt close to where he stood.

"How are things underground?" Lassen called back. His

wife shut down her skip and dismounted before answering. She had been keeping an eye on the mining operation while he and Jihrmar prepared for the march.

"The miners you haven't recruited for the military don't have much of a heart for working—everyone knows something is happening, and the rumors are flying like seeds from a Jambwa tree in spring."

"That's fine," Lassen assured his aide. "The more versions of this story there are, the harder it will be for our enemies to glean the truth from whatever they hear."

"It looks like quite a force to me," commended Lassen's wife admiringly.

"I think we've done well. We have about 25 armored Valorians—they are the largest, strongest, most disciplined men of our land, and they are plated with polished coblatium to deflect anything but a direct hit from a shoulder blaster. When the battle starts, they'll go ahead of the other troops along the enemy's front line to find a weak spot. When they do, they'll concentrate on that area until it's broken. The rest of us will drive through like a wedge. If we are able to continue, we'll fight our way right into Wyntir and onto the steps of the government center. Our marksmen will be interspersed at regular and strategic areas of the assault. We have armored troop carriers that will be able to scale any barriers they try to erect against us."

"How are the other nations' preparations?"

"I understand they are going well, but for security reasons we have not shared any details with each other."

"I suppose I can't blame them," she said. "How prepared are we?"

Lassen smiled gently.

"We're as ready as anyone can be for this. I keep hoping that something will happen, that someone will do something that will make this attack unnecessary, but here we are, only a day away from the beginning."

Lassen's wife stared at the ground, sharing his hopes.

"I've been thinking that there must be some god, some being with more sense than we have, and with more power over our destinies," said Lassen. "I have been praying to it of late."

"I hope it helps," she said quietly. Then, forcing herself to a more energetic tone of voice, she continued. "I need you to tell me what else we need for the operation's Restoration bunker. You know, staffing and supplies and the like. It won't take long—I have it all organized in a list."

"That sounds like the woman I married. With any luck you'll be bored back here because there will be no casualties to send you. But let's hear the list."

Keneche slammed the dusty book and hurled it at the bookshelf in disgust. He had spent a day and a half searching the archives for plans or descriptions that might reveal some dungeon or cell that he had not searched. He had scoured every abandoned or unused room, tower and closet in the government center for days and found no trace of Altua—yet from what he could piece together from the scant information provided by talkative staff who had heard the commotion the night Altua disappeared, Keneche firmly believed the aged ambassador was being held in or near the government center.

In the days during his search, Keneche had learned that Altua had come to the government center some time ago, probably to object to the treatment and discrimination against the natives on Neece. He had confronted several delegates and military officials, and had even confronted Keneche's father. As an ambassador, he commanded attention and hospitality, but after he was there for several days he was no longer seen.

Keneche sat on the second rung of the ladder used to shelve books near the ceiling, and he looked at the volumes scattered on the floor. As the time drew closer to the tenth and final day of his agreement with Lam Laeo, he began to grow desperate and simply dropped each book or collection of papers with no information. Now it was day ten. He had searched all night, knowing that if he did not find out where Altua was imprisoned by the time his friend started his shift, he would not get the master key in time and he would not get to Lam in time. Lam would then be under no obligation to keep his identity secret from Brakan. Maybe this would not be a problem, but from what Keneche was learning about the time Braken and Kruge spent together, he strongly suspected it was.

Keneche hung his weary head in his hands and reviewed his options. He had already talked to everyone he dared, he had scoured the archives, he had physically searched the government center. The only thing he had not done was pray to the gods, although he was fairly certain that none of their gods would be interested in his particular problem.

But what about Altua's God? wondered Keneche suddenly. *Altua said he was quite powerful, and quite caring—perhaps he would be interested in helping me find Altua.*

Keneche was not sure how to address the Source, but he thought he should lie on the floor, so he flattened himself against the dusty tile and repressed a sneeze.

"God of Altua," Keneche began haltingly, "I know you are a powerful God, and a caring God. Altua even called you the 'Source' and the 'Power.' Surely you would be interested in Altua's safety. I need your help to find him—I am desperate and know of nowhere else to turn."

Keneche was silent, waiting for a revelation or a sign, but nothing stirred, not even the dust.

"I have nothing to offer you—I don't even know what you require for favors, but I am willing to give you the credit when he is found," Keneche bargained. Still nothing, except that even though lying on the floor felt good after being up all night, he had the urge to raise his head and look over the shelves one last time.

He raised his eyes to the bottom shelf. In front of it he could see the last book he had searched and then thrown in his frustration. It had apparently knocked several others from the shelf when it hit. He looked up to see the space it had left. It was in a section on the financial histories, so he had not bothered to look there before.

A golden gleam shone from the space behind one of the books he had knocked off. Keneche raised himself farther from the ground and saw that it was some sort of object hidden behind the volumes on that shelf.

Keneche leaped to his feet and hastily plowed off the other books in front of it. The gleaming object was a leather box with golden hinges, feet, and corners—and a lock. He pulled the long container from the shelf and placed it on the floor. Taking careful aim with his antique Redlyn pistol, he pulled the activator. Nothing happened. He angrily slapped the pistol grip and shook it— a trick he used many times to renew the worn connections with the Redlyn supply. He aimed again, and this time a brilliant red flash exploded the lock, as well as a few floor tiles beneath the box.

Not waiting for it to cool, he tore at the fragmented lock and blew on his fingers in between attempts. Finally it fell off and he pried open the lid. His heart raced and his hands trembled as they delved into the box. The box had concealed a long roll of parchment—the kind that building designs were written on.

He weighted down one end of the parchment with the box and gently uncurled the brittle paper. As he worked, floor after floor of the government center unrolled. As he ran out of parchment, he saw the bottom floor and recognized on it the archives he was now in, the skip port and the utility room—and something else he found very intriguing. Off the utility room was a short tunnel and then some small rooms marked "storage"—of what it didn't suggest. Past the rooms was another tunnel that ended in dotted lines labeled "storm sewer."

Keneche trembled as he rolled up the paper. No one knew of this room—the entrance must be hidden. A conviction grew in him that Altua was hidden there, and tonight he would have a key. Suddenly realizing the disgraceful condition of the archives, he quickly straightened it in case someone bothered to look there and get suspicious. He couldn't afford to take chances until tonight—and then he would have only one.

Chapter Fourteen

Keneche fingered the precious master key as he felt his way to the back of the dark water room in the lowest level of the government center. He felt the heat from the water tanks, and heard the hissing and knocking of the purifiers. A soft blue glow from the M-stone amulet around his neck at least kept him from tripping on pipes. He could not tell if it was brighter or if it just seemed so because of the lack of other light.

He groped along a row of pipes he hoped would take him to the end of the room, a journey that seemed endless.

"This is certainly a good hiding place," Keneche said out loud just to hear something other than the machinery that droned in his ears.

When he was beginning to wonder if the pipes were just leading him in a circle around the room over and over, his fingers ran into a valve. He felt the pipes above and below it—most of them had valves. He let go of the pipe and reached out ahead of him. A wall.

With a sense of relief, he began to look for a crack in the wall. He started at the pipes and worked his way along the wall. He found rusted inscriptions, flaking paint, row after row of mildewed block, and finally, a line which ran from the floor to the ceiling. He walked a little farther and found another line. With mounting excitement, he searched the right side of what he now believed to be the door he hoped would lead him to Altua. Shortly, his diligence rewarded him with the discovery of a small metal disk set into the block.

The dampness, heat and chemicals in the room had badly rusted the disk, and he hoped that the mechanism still functioned. If Altua was there, it would certainly be in working order.

Hesitating at first, Keneche pressed the master key card against the disk. For a moment nothing happened; then he heard a click and the door began to swing open toward him. Keneche smiled at his success and hurried around the door into the tunnel it used to conceal.

As he crept along the tunnel, he examined the rounded walls for signs of doors, but he knew they were supposed to be deeper in. The features of the tunnel appeared indistinct in the dim M-stone light, as if they were lit by Elna, the moon. But he was pleased to find the tunnel dry and, as far as he could see, devoid of jealous creatures.

"Ow!" he whispered out loud as his toe connected sharply with a metal grate that spanned the tunnel. He had been using his light on the wall and had not seen the obstruction in his way. He groped along and found that it completely blocked the tunnel. However, he did find a key card button. Keneche quickly retrieved the master key from his pocket, held it to the button and waited for the click of the opening lock. Instead, alarms sounded.

The high-pitched waves of the siren pierced his ears and he stood stunned for a moment. This was certainly not in his plan. Red lights flashed above him. Lights snapped on and flooded the tunnel.

At least I'll be able to see, Keneche thought to himself, *and I won't have to be quiet.* With that not-very-comforting thought in mind, he drew his Redlyn pistol and loosed a red bolt at the lock on the grate. Sparks flew, and some molten metal dripped down the lock at the bolt's impact. One more shot and Keneche was able to rattle open the door of the gate.

Keneche looked back as he stepped through the bars. What he saw made his jaw drop and his hand grope again for his pistol, clipped to his belt for easy access. A defense drone, alerted by the alarm he had triggered, floated into the tunnel behind him. It was a red and black cylinder with several infrared lenses and a swiveling weapon on its bottom end which erupted into red fire when it detected Keneche.

He dropped to the floor and flattened himself against the wall and returned the fire. His first volley simply bit into the metal grate as did the fire the defense drone loosed. The bars became red hot as Redlyn bolts laced the air in a furious exchange of fire.

Keneche finally struck the drone and smashed one of its lenses. It swiveled around attempting to compensate, and while it was temporarily occupied with that, Keneche scrambled down the tunnel. Keneche knew he had only moments before the drone oriented itself and followed him through the gate. The rooms were there, and he tried two doors, which were not locked—he decided not to check them, assuming Altua's cell would be locked. By now he was sure that Altua was down there. There certainly wouldn't be restricted locks and defense drones to guard ancient junk rooms.

A locked door. Keneche wasted no time in shattering it with Redlyn fire and storming into the dark room. In the corner was the pathetic form of an old man, blinking dumbfoundedly because of the light, much of which came from the now-brilliant M-stones they both wore. Keneche fired again at the chain that bound the man who was obviously Altua; then he ran to help him up.

"You feel more solid than a dream," the old man croaked weakly. "And you wear an M-stone."

"I'm no dream," said Keneche breathlessly as he hoisted Altua to his feet and put the ambassador's arm around his shoulder so he could help him walk. "I'm a friend come to take you to safety." To himself, Keneche wondered that the gaunt figure beside him could still be living.

"I did not think I was called to the Other Side just yet," said Altua.

Keneche nearly had to drag his treasure to the cell's doorway. Without looking he raised his weapon then entered the tunnel shooting. The drone was waiting and returned the fire, filling the tunnel with screaming echoes and shattering pieces of tile. Sprays of dust clouded the tunnel. The drone fled behind one of the doors Keneche had opened while testing locks, and Keneche took advantage of the dust-clouded tunnel and the lull in the exchange to hoist Altua into the tunnel and stumble away from the drone.

Another grate faced them almost immediately, but Keneche did not hesitate to slice it open and push Altua through. As he followed, he heard the whir the defense drone's lenses made as they rotated, searching for the infrared readings that their bodies emitted. Keneche swallowed his panic and willed his trembling limbs forward. The hot bars of the grate the two men had just crawled through confused the drone for a moment, long enough for Keneche to shoot first. His bolt glanced off the drone's reflective surface and it flew to a more defensible position and returned the fire.

Keneche had studied the map of the tunnel, and he already planned his escape. One area in the floor of the tunnel led to the storm sewers, and he directed his Redlyn fire at that spot to make an opening large enough for the men. The bolts split the air and cracked the concrete as they hit. Two more shots and enough had crumbled to let Keneche drop to the rubble in the sewer tunnel below.

Altua crawled after him, and when Keneche had helped him down, they struck off down the new route. Again they gained a few moments as the drone's circuits evaluated the new wrinkle in the chase and determined to pursue its target. It moved to the hole in the floor and examined it; then it blasted it a bit larger so that it could fit through and lowered itself down. Keneche and Altua were not to be detected, but the almost imperceptible glow of infrared radiation from their hands on the wall showed the drone which direction to go. Its lenses swiveled and its weapon extended and prepared to fire when it detected the forms again.

Keneche stumbled and fell to one knee; the water splashed to his hip as he supported Altua and kept him from collapsing in the water.

"Leave me and save yourself," Altua urged.

"Shh, save your strength," the boy reprimanded as he struggled to his feet with his charge. "I'm not doing this for the adventure—I'm not about to leave you here."

The two splashed down a turn in the tunnel, Keneche running through the route in his mind, hoping he knew where they were as they trudged in the darkness. The splashing and running water, combined with the echoes, kept him from hearing if they were being followed, but he knew they must be. He would rather have confronted it head-on than wonder if it were two paces behind ready to pierce them through.

Keneche stopped suddenly. Not far behind them he finally heard the whirring of the defense drone. Keneche swung around and fired several rounds down the tunnel. The bright flashes illuminated the tunnel for a moment, but he could see no pursuer. As the echoes of his volley died, he again heard the whirr.

"It's there," muttered Keneche. "And it has the advantage—it can see in the dark."

"Why have we stopped?" asked Altua feebly.

"I'm feeling the wall—there's supposed to be a way out," responded Keneche, panic leaking into his voice.

"The Source might call us to lay down our lives, but he never deceives us into believing there is a way out when there isn't," Altua assured his youthful rescuer.

Keneche continued frantically searching the wall for the marks that told him the way out, ignoring the strange speech of the man. *He's delirious from malnutrition*, Keneche thought.

"Keneche?" A voice called from farther down the tunnel.

"Coming!" shouted Keneche. "We aren't far enough," he explained breathlessly as he half-dragged Altua toward the sound of his friend's voice.

Keneche's legs were cramped from the cold water, and his side ached from running and supporting Altua. He knew they didn't have far to go, but it was still too close to the drone's blaster. He stumbled forward as he heard a bolt scream through the air and slam into the tunnel wall behind them just as they rounded a corner and was hit in the back with debris from the impact. Then they saw it.

"Light!" Keneche exclaimed. Light from the hiding place poured through the open hatch, and one of Cruzan's disciples waited on the ladder to help them up. Keneche handed Altua off to less fatigued hands and hurled around to keep the metal monster at bay. Red bolts traced scars into the stone and filled the tunnel with the sounds of battle. The drone was programmed to be bold, and it was not intimidated by Keneche's aggression.

Keneche fired one last round into the dark tunnel, leaped

to the rungs, and pulled himself up. As he passed a service ledge in the shaft a child of 11 waited excitedly to execute his role in the battle.

"Now!" Keneche said as he flew up the ladder. The boy tugged on the ancient equipment they had recently prepared for the job and a low knocking began to vibrate through the tunnel; then a rushing sound coursed through the pipes. Moments later, water began to belch out of the main, flooding the tunnel almost instantly. Keneche smiled to himself as he pictured the drone's lenses spinning wildly, trying to escape the rising waters until it seeped into its casing and blew apart its circuits from the inside.

Keneche heaved himself onto the floor of the converted control room and lay there dripping, aching, exhausted.

It wasn't long before he was wrapped in a blanket and sipping some of the brew he had brought them only a few days ago.

Altua was propped up in a bed, gratefully taking the soup Keneche's mother spooned into him.

"Thank you for being used of the Power to free me," Altua said for about the fifth time.

"Your safety is thanks enough," Keneche assured him. "Now I have to catch up with Lam Laeo. You are in no condition to travel, so I'll leave you in their care here and try to bring Lam to you."

"Whatever you think best," agreed Altua, still barely able to believe he was really free and eating—he had had many such hallucinations while in his dark cell.

Cruzan stood near his grandson, Keneche, with folded arms. Hearing the account of the ambassador's rescue made him even more discontented with his self-imposed imprisonment. Part of the Valorian discipline was knowing the meaning behind words, and Cruzan knew for a long time that Kruge intended to be master of the solar system. Cruzan made his opposition statement to force Kruge's hand.

"I do not feel right letting a boy risk his life and carry on all these dangerous plans while I sit idly in this room."

"You have not sat or been idle since we came here, Papa," Keneche's mother scolded.

"This boy is doing fine," said Keneche, trying not to sound too disrespectful. "You'll be needed soon enough, I'll bet, and you must be safe until then."

"I just wanted you to know I don't enjoy this life of ease," Cruzan told him with a wink.

"I just hope Lam hasn't talked to Brakan yet," mused Keneche, not necessarily intending anyone to hear.

"Brakan?" Altua croaked, wrestling his weak body into a sitting position. "I don't know this Lam that my planet sent, but I hope he is not mixed up with Brakan."

"Lam came here to find you, but on the way he was captured on Elna. Brakan, as you probably know, is the moon-base commander. He told Lam he was part of an underground conspiracy against Kruge—a conspiracy I am a part of, although it has been a very small one until recently. I have been Brakan's agent in the government center, but I never allowed him to learn my identity—I guess I don't completely trust him."

"You are a good judge of character, young man," Altua said. "I came from Neece a while ago—I don't know how long since I have been in that windowless prison. I came to protest to the Council of Delegates the treatment the Be'Nay were receiving from the settlers, and from the Vassirians, for that matter. They put up with me for a while, at one point even asked me to be an agent for them on Neece, to keep them appraised of the settlers' attitudes and activities. I refused, of course, and they eventually locked me up—by then I knew too much."

Keneche put down his drink on the pavement under the pipes and leaned forward to study the man's answer to the question that burned in his mind.

"Who are 'they'?" Keneche asked in a whisper. Altua pulled on his matted beard a bit as he thought of the best way to present it to Keneche.

"Kruge, of course," Altua began. "And Brakan was part of that group, as you've probably guessed by now—oh, yes, and Bolog, the Woodlander."

Keneche paled and began to tremble.

"You are sure of what you say?" Keneche managed to ask.

"My son, Brakan, Bolog and your father had more schemes

than I could keep track of. I got the impression they wanted no one to know they were working together so closely, thinking they could get more information that way—just as they wanted me to do for them."

"Do you know what this means?" Keneche asked weakly. "Lam is Brakan's puppet and is in grave danger. If he tells Brakan what he wants to know, so am I. But that is the least of our troubles. Bolog and Lassen, a former delegate from Redland, have allied themselves against my father and Highland. I helped coordinate the communication between allies. If Bolog is allied with my father and Brakan, then . . ." Keneche could not bring himself to describe the ramifications. Cruzan finished his sentence for him.

"Lassen's forces are marching into an ambush."

Chapter Fifteen

Dawn came early in Redland. The sky was just beginning to lighten, and the dark forms of night feeders could be seen against it, winging their way home after a night of foraging.

This is always the coldest part of the day. Lassen shivered and pulled his cloak tighter. The climate in Redland was very mild, and it really wasn't all that cold. Perhaps it was the dampness of the mist that rose up around them that made Lassen shudder, or perhaps it was just the dread of the mission that lay before them.

Lassen, along with Jihrmar, some other officers and troops, stood on the flatbed of a large transport with a plasma bolt thrower mounted on the front. The entire platform rested about half a man's height from the ground, suspended in the air by gravity resistors that hummed quietly. In the few moments before they were ready to leave, Lassen gazed at his city, sleeping in the cold morning mist. He loved the people there—his family, friends, workers. He loved the buildings and the work done there. He loved Redland, and no one would take those things from him—from the people of Redland.

He glanced behind them and saw that the sky was beginning to show some color—red and deep orange just above the horizon.

They say a red sky in the morning is a bad omen, Lassen told himself. *Good thing I don't believe in omens.*

When he turned back toward the town, he saw a figure fast approaching on a skip. He knew it would be his wife. Along with Keneche, she was one of the few nonmilitary people who knew they were leaving that morning. The militia itself had not known this would be the day until a few hours ago.

It was indeed Lassen's wife, and when she had dismounted her skip, she ran to the transport to be greeted by Lassen's tender kiss.

"How are the children?" Lassen asked.

"They're fine," she answered, attempting to be casual, but not covering her distress very well. "Little Innis asked where you were last night. I told her you were working and would not be back for a few days." She bit her lip, struggling to be calm.

Lassen nodded and then tried to assure her.

"This will be a short campaign. I'll see all of you again in a few days."

She nodded this time, but she was losing her battle against her tears.

"The first night we'll be spending in south central Seaward where the Seaward and Sundor militias will join us. We plan to travel along the Tempest ocean coast to the northernmost corner of Woodland by the next afternoon where we'll join the Woodland militia. We'll rest until nightfall and then march into Highland. If they are as surprised and frightened by our show of force as we hope, it will be over soon."

"And if not?" Lassen's wife managed to squeeze out of her throat.

Lassen knelt down on the edge of the transport to be as close as possible to his wife.

"It will be over soon, and I'll be back," he assured her. She straightened the collar of his cloak and polished the already-shiny clasp with the heal of her hand.

"Good," she said. "You look so handsome in your uniform. I miss you already."

Lassen leaned over and wrapped his arms around her, and she no longer bothered to fight her tears. She buried her face in her husband's shoulder and he comforted her by stroking her hair as she sobbed. He quickly brushed the tears from his own eyes before he gently pushed her back.

"We're leaving now."

"Somewhere I hope there is a god who will hear my prayers for you," she said as she turned and took a few steps to her skip. She turned back and said the words she wanted him to hear last, the words she hoped would stay with him as they marched: "I love you."

"I love you, too," Lassen said, smiling as she turned and ran for her skip.

He watched her speed off to the city, and when he could see her no longer, he turned to Jihrmar. Lassen swallowed hard and rubbed his nose, trying to appear cool and unaffected, but he knew the results of his efforts were poor, that it was a waste of strength.

"There is a good chance we will be successful—we are four poorly equipped armies against one well-equipped. We also have the surprise advantage."

"But there is a good chance we won't . . ." Lassen began, adding the "but" that the commander had left out.

"If you already feel defeated, we don't even have a chance," Jihrmar admonished.

"Of course, you're right. I just think of the investment we've made in this action. Not only the tremendous expense in resources, but the effort we've put into maintaining security. It hasn't been easy checking all our plans with an adolescent on the other side of the continent, especially when he's so secretive about what he plans on doing in Wyntir."

"You understand that this fight was inevitable," Jihrmar reasoned. "We either had to let them come here and trample our homeland as they fought us, or meet them on their own territory where they will be hesitant to use their most destructive weapons for fear of killing their own people and destroying their own homeland."

"Yes," admitted Lassen. "And if we are successful, we will be the new rulers of a bitter and bankrupt planet. If we lose, we lose our lives."

"Just think of what you want for Vassir, and we will win it for her."

A lone shout went up, and several horns sounded from the corners of the column of transports. Overhead, several large, black fighters roared past, the six landing legs on each retracting into their hulls, and the transports began to move. Despite the heavy atmosphere, a cheer went up from the soldiers. Each one's face showed dread, but that intense emotion mingled with the excitement of the impending battle. The excitement encouraged Lassen, and he allowed himself a smile as he turned his back to his city and faced Seaward.

Kruge's lank form towered in the entryway to the small dining room near the government-center kitchen.

"I knew I'd find you with the food, Bolog," he said, startling the rotund delegate. Bolog quickly swallowed and wiped his greasy hands on the napkin tucked beneath his chins.

"What did you want?" Bolog asked after swallowing.

"There is a disturbing wrinkle I wish to discuss," said Kruge, storming into the room and pulling up a chair near Bolog. "Altua is gone. Someone has broken into his cell, defeated the defense drone, and escaped."

"What does this mean?" asked Bolog worriedly.

"It means that whoever is Brakan's contact in the government center is well informed, and, if Altua was in any condition to speak, is probably even better informed by now—although we intend to discover his contact's identity very soon."

"It doesn't matter," decided Bolog, snatching a glass of bubbling wine. "Your Highland army is already at the border of Woodland. The pitiful militias of Redland, Seaward, and Sundor will join my militia, and when they step into Highland, they will be surprised to face two enemies—not only Highland, but also Woodland from within their own ranks. It will be all over in moments, probably with little bloodshed, and you'll be a hero."

"It is too bad that your head is not as well-endowed as your belly," quipped Kruge sharply. "Altua's escape is a critical problem. I am sending my own Valorians to monitor the situation from the air."

"What will they do if our plans have failed?" asked Bolog critically.

Kruge looked at Bolog with his ashen eyes and hissed cooly. "Whatever is necessary."

Bolog was ready to take another mouthful of fowl, but when he heard Kruge's extreme intentions, he suddenly lost his appetite. Bolog dropped his fork and fidgeted under Kruge's oppressive stare.

The bench was wet with dew, but it was too early in the morning for standing, and Lam had parked his skip too far away to walk back. He brushed off the moisture as best he could with his hand, then sat down and looked out over the rushing river.

The wooden bench was fastened to the planks of the pier beside the river. Behind him was a park, and at his feet was the river—not nearly as quiet here near Port Cloud as it was through Travalia.

As he sat and waited for Brakan, he thought about what Aba had said to Lista and him the night before.

"The 'health' team is supposed to come in a few days," Aba had said needlessly. "We don't know what will happen to us. But your danger is certain—you are fugitives and may be shot on sight." Subdued lighting cast a pensive glow on their faces. Aba pushed a lever on his own chair and he hummed closer to Lista. "My dear, I care about you too much for that; Lam, this is not your struggle. I think both of you should flee while you have the chance."

Lista had flung her arms around the elderly leader.

"And where would I go that I wouldn't worry myself to death wondering about you all?" scolded Lista.

"I'm staying, too," Lam announced. "There are two more chances I have to postpone the inspection. A Highland Government Center servant is supposed to contact me by tomorrow. Also, a high-ranking Highland officer is meeting me at dawn tomorrow in Port Cloud—I'm hoping one of those men can help us."

Lam remembered how Aba had fixed his knowing gaze on Lam and asked, "Why do you even care about us? Even our fellow Vassirians don't care—and you're an alien."

"I may be an alien," Lam conceded, "but we both have the same Source. I've gotten myself in too deep to ignore that—even though as a servant of the Source, the Power, and the Friend, I'm about as much good as a skip without gravity resistors."

As Lam sat in the coolness of the pre-dawn and on the dampness of his wooden lookout, he realized how remarkable it was that his words had an impact on Aba and Lista. Aba insisted on hearing more when things settled down. But what was remarkable was that they were moved even though Lam felt about as much like a follower of the Way of Tsu as Chairman Kruge at the moment. He had kicked and rebelled and been bitter and even refused to talk to the Friend. He felt very distant from the Source, and hoped that it wasn't too late.

"Friend," he whispered, "I don't know if you're around anymore. I've been sort of busy and we haven't talked for a while. I guess I wouldn't blame you if you're angry."

This sounds dumb, he thought to himself. *How do I start? How do we get comfortable again?*

Lam looked up from his inward struggle for a moment and saw a man with a cloak wrapped around him, his back to Lam, leaning against a pole with a pulley used for unloading river-boats.

"Brakan?" Lam called. The figure turned slowly and even in the dim mist, Lam could tell that the white hair belonged to the commander of the moon base.

"And what is it that couldn't wait?" asked Brakan in an impatient tone.

"Are you aware of plans to harm any Travalians?" asked Lam when he had risen from his bench and joined Brakan on the pier by the river.

Brakan looked thoughtful for a moment, and then answered noncommittally, "Not directly, but I know that such things have been discussed generally. Why do you care?"

"Why is it so surprising that I would care what happens to my friends?" Lam asked angrily.

"I'll look into it and see what I can do," Brakan said distantly. Lam thought that he should feel more relieved than he was, and was about to demand a description of what Brakan intended on doing, but Brakan had questions of his own.

"So what is your appraisal of my government-center contact?" Brakan asked.

"We had a bargain," said Lam. "He didn't prove himself to me, I guess."

"Perhaps it is just a communication problem," said Brakan diplomatically, "which is why I wanted you to find out who he was—we need more direct communication. Things are heating up and we have to take advantage of opportunities against Kruge swiftly when we get a chance."

Lam thought for a moment. He didn't feel quite right telling Brakan about Keneche, but then Brakan upheld his bargain—he freed Lam and Lista from Highland Government Center. Keneche, on the other hand, did not show up with Altua. *Keneche is just a teenager,* Lam reasoned with himself. *Maybe he needs more direct supervision like he would receive under Brakan.*

"Your contact is Keneche Krugeson," Lam said. He instantly regretted it.

"Keneche," Brakan repeated, smiling slyly. "That explains much. Who would have thought that one of Kruge's own sons—"

"So what's next?" asked Lam nervously. Brakan's answers shocked him.

"Thank you for your assistance," spat Brakan sarcastically as he pulled a Redlyn pistol from beneath his cloak. "You have won your place in the history of the new Vassir."

Lam stared at the pistol point aimed for his midsection and knew there was nothing he could do.

Lam's face was not the only one to wear a shocked expression. Keneche had run from the storm sewer outlet near the river to his mother's apartment near the government center. Although he was breaking curfew and violating the vehicle laws by taking his skip at night, he had decided that it didn't matter much compared with the damage he had already done.

Keneche had raced to Travalia and awakened Aba to find out where Lam was. When Keneche finally got to the pier, it was morning twilight, and he saw he was too late to warn Lam. He watched from behind some potted plants as he drew out his pistol and pre-activated it.

When Brakan pulled his weapon on Lam, Keneche was tempted to take a shot at the traitor, but he could also see that farther down the pier, near the shore behind a small building, there was a Highland soldier crouching behind his skip, aiming a shoulder blaster with infrared light beam sighting at Lam.

"So Brakan's not only a liar, he's a coward," Keneche muttered under his breath.

Keneche knew that if he managed to shoot either Brakan or the soldier, the other would kill Lam—and then come after him. The direct approach would not work, so he tucked his pistol in the neck of his tunic, quietly slipped to the edge of the pier and lowered himself into the water.

Lam first tried to decide whether to turn and run or lunge at Brakan's neck and break it, no matter what the consequences might be. Instead, he inwardly gasped a prayer, asking the Power for direction and protection.

"How do you know everything I just told you has not been a lie?" asked Lam, appearing fairly calm, under the circumstances. Brakan's wild eyes narrowed for a moment as he considered the possibility.

"It doesn't matter," Brakan said, his white hair looking like a blizzard in the wind. "This evening it will all be over, anyway. The armies of Redland, Seaward and Sundor will be conquered tonight when they march on Highland. Not only is our army waiting for them, Woodland will turn on them at the same time—an ambush from within!"

"Do you think that will really work?" asked Lam harshly, stalling for time.

"I am the one that devised this whole military aspect of the Operation Master Planet. Of course it will work!"

"That is your name for Kruge's scheme?" Lam continued to stall, not really listening to the answers, but trying to devise a plan to escape or overcome Brakan.

"Ha!" Brakan laughed insultingly. "Those reforms are only a prelude. We planned that the worthless troublemakers in Redland and the other nations would attack, and we plan to squash them under Highland's heel, just as the stones are ground into dust by Highland's great mountains. Then the way will be clear for us to lead Vassir into a new age of glory!"

Keneche pulled himself along the edge of the pier, out of sight and in water up to his armpits. The water chilled him, and the current tugged at him steadily, but he managed to keep his hold and inch closer to Brakan's backup marksman. When he reached the spot on the pier just beyond the building where the marksman crouched, Keneche heaved himself up slowly, trying to avoid splashes that might attract attention. His arms shook from the exertion, but he finally made it out of the water and lay on the wooden slats in a puddle of river water. A stack of crates scattered on the pier provided Keneche with perfect cover to creep along the boards to the shore, dripping as he stalked.

Keneche cautiously regarded the building that sheltered Brakan's backup to make sure he was still hidden as he drew the narrow blade from the sheath on his left boot. A light pillar like those he maintained at the government center rose from the ground in front of him, and Keneche lay in the flower bed at the base and pried open the plate from the control panel. He reached inside and groped for the coil of wire he knew would be there, pulled out the power connections, and yanked out the spool. He hoped Brakan and his shadow would assume the light pillar shut off automatically as the light of dawn increased.

When he had wound a nice coil of the wire, Keneche crouched crate-high and made his way through the piled cargo to the marksman's skip. When Keneche peered anxiously over the top of the last crate and saw that Brakan's soldier was totally absorbed in watching Lam and Brakan, he tied a quick slipknot in the end of the flexible wire and secured it to the skip's speed toggle. The other end he poked through the slots in the pier's boards. Keneche then slipped back to the water's edge and again lowered himself into the current.

"You've stalled long enough!" snapped Brakan. "Move over to the river edge of the pier."

"I don't think so," Lam responded brashly. "If I die, I want you to have to drag me to the edge and throw me in—I won't do your work for you."

Brakan scowled for a moment, and then shrugged, raising his weapon higher and aiming it at Lam's chest. Lam stared at the point, knowing that a fiery bolt of red energy would erupt from it and end his life—and there was nothing he could do about it. A strange sense of peace welled up inside Lam, and somehow he felt ready—ready to meet the Friend face-to-face. The feeling surprised him—he was sure he would feel panic, or at least anger.

Keneche had pulled himself along underneath the pier so

that he was positioned between the soldier and Brakan. He uncoiled the wire until he had a loop which he pushed through the slit between the boards in the pier. The other end of the wire ran along underneath the pier, up through a slit and was attached to the speed control of the soldier's skip.

Holding onto the boards above him with one hand, Keneche hurried as fast as he could with his free hand. He knew that one mistake and everything would be lost—Lam's life, his own life, and the armies that would be ambushed by Highland and Woodland. It was not a comforting thought, so he pushed it from his mind and absorbed himself in directing his trembling fingers. He could not hear the words discussed above him, but by the tone he knew time was short.

Keneche took a deep breath, then pulled in the slack wire attached to the marksman's skip. He heard its engine start to wind up.

The vigilant soldier dropped his guard when he saw his skip start to move by itself. It glided slowly toward Lam and Brakan, then started to speed up and spin in tight circles. In a panic, the soldier holstered his blaster and ran to corral his vehicle. He would have made it, too, except that he didn't see a wire loop suddenly spring up through the space between the boards in the pier. He caught his right foot in the loop and crashed to the boards as he felt the loop tighten around his ankle into a knot.

The commotion immediately drew Brakan's attention. "What is this?" Brakan demanded frantically. As soon as Brakan turned to look at the antics of his once-professional and disciplined backup, Lam lunged at Brakan and grabbed his gun wrist. Brakan was so surprised, and Lam's grip so tight, that the Redlyn pistol slipped from his hand and clattered onto the boards.

The helpless soldier could not reach his own weapon because the wildly spinning skip was attached to his leg, dragging him with it on its reckless course. Keneche was almost too excited to find the strength to pull himself back up on the pier and join the fray. But he managed, and slipping only occasionally on his wet boots, he chased after the soldier, hoping to disarm him.

Brakan leaned over to grab his pistol, but Lam had his knee ready to greet Brakan's jaw. He stumbled back and Lam had just enough time to kick the pistol into the river. The moon-base commander watched in horror as his weapon made ripples in the water and slowly sank, carried downstream by the current.

"No, get back!" Brakan yelled. Lam walked toward him slowly and Brakan looked anxiously to each side. Lam would be able to catch him if he ran to either side, and behind him was the Snowy River. Like an animal with no escape from a predator, Brakan lunged at Lam, screaming. Lam grabbed his attacker's arm and pulled, using Brakan's momentum against him.

Brakan crashed on the boards from Lam's throw, then staggered to his feet. Lam delivered a quick blow to Brakan's midsection before he straightened, and he doubled over and gasped for breath. Calling all the little-used discipline trained into him long ago, Brakan managed his own swing that caught Lam by surprise as it connected with his side. It hurt, but it didn't incapacitate him, and Lam cracked his fist against Brakan's jaw, sending him staggering back, dangerously close to the edge of the pier.

Waving his arms to keep his balance did not help Brakan, and he fell into the water, still flapping his arms like a wounded bird. Lam watched the once-dignified military leader struggle to keep his head above the rushing water.

"Now I'm not so sure about those ribs, Lista," Lam groaned, holding his side.

When Lam looked back to the action on the pier, Keneche was still chasing the soldier who was being dragged by the wild skip. The tremendous sense of relief Lam felt made the scene even more amusing, and all he could do was laugh in spite of his pain.

"The least you could do is give me a hand here," Keneche pleaded breathlessly.

Lam pulled himself together enough to pull out his own pistol and train it on the moving target.

"You catch the skip," Lam advised, still chuckling.

The two of them soon had the skip controlled and the soldier bound and slung over the skip Lam had taken from Travalia.

"You promised me an ambassador, son," Lam reminded Keneche as soon as they had things under reasonable control.

"I have good news," Keneche announced as he tightened the wire behind the soldier's wrists. "I found Altua and delivered him safely to the care of some friends of mine. As soon as we have time, I'll tell you exactly what I went through, too."

Lam stopped and looked at Keneche.

"You found him?"

"You look shocked."

"That was my mission here—and now you're telling me it's over."

Keneche glared at Lam, trying to decide what his intentions were.

"You've no obligation to us," he said coldly. "I can arrange for you and Altua to go to a friendlier region. I don't know how you'll get off the planet, but you're clever—"

"Stop it, Ken," Lam said, grabbing the youth by the shoulders. "It's just hard to believe that he's found and safe. And I guess I always planned on having something to do with it."

Keneche grinned at Lam.

"I have another mission now," Lam continued. "There are some people not far from here who saved my life, and I'd like to return the favor. Your fight is mine, partner."

The two shook hands to seal their partnership and then got back to business.

"What did Brakan tell you about the ambush?" asked Keneche.

"I don't know any of the details, but it sounds like Redland, Seaward and another nation I don't remember were going to be attacked by Woodland and Highland."

"Where?" Keneche demanded, eager to have this new source of information.

"As soon as they march on Highland this evening," Lam said, realizing the urgency of the situation.

Keneche stood silently for a moment, lost in concentration. Lam looked at him anxiously and the soldier eyed him hatefully—the gag in his mouth was probably the only thing that kept him from spitting at the boy.

"Altua was the one who warned me that Brakan and Bolog, the delegate to the Council from Woodland, were conspiring with my father. What you say confirms it. The militias of Redland, Seaward and Sundor are marching to join Woodland's militia—they think they are allies, but they will be taken by surprise and maybe killed as soon as they cross into Highland."

"Can we warn them by com-link?" Lam offered.

"Too risky," Keneche dismissed. "I'm sure that every frequency is being monitored right now. But somehow we have to warn them before they get here to Woodland."

Lam had been leaning on the skip, the morning sun starting to warm his chilled skin. As the sun began to dawn, so did an uncanny feeling that there must be more they could do.

"I think we can turn this whole thing around," Lam said, barely controlling his excitement. "But we'll need the help of some friends of mine not too far from here."

Lam climbed stiffly onto his skip and motioned for Keneche to do the same. Keneche bent down to the soldier's skip and snapped out the Redlyn rod cartridge. The heavy and expensive power supply was probably much newer than his own.

After switching cartridges, Keneche pulled up his skip behind Lam and their prisoner. They would leave the soldier's skip behind.

"Either I have a good idea, or I'm insane," Lam called back to Keneche. "I'll tell you what I think we can do on the way to Travalia."

Chapter Sixteen

Chairman Kruge's restless mind kept him awake all night. He finally gave up on his hope of sleep and left his favorite wife in her apartment.

Kruge, in his study with the shades drawn where he had been most of the night, only vaguely recognized that dawn was breaking. Over and over he analyzed the situation.

"Why are they fighting me on this?" Kruge's whispered demand hissed into the air. He sat motionless, staring with dry eyes at the Vassirian flag displayed on the wall and waited for an answer, but the air was still.

Nothing in Kruge's stony expression revealed the object of his concentration, but his red-rimmed eyes periodically narrowed to fierce slits. Kruge spun the large Vassirian globe near his desk with one finger, as he did often to give his hands something to do while he thought. He watched the oceans and the main lands pass before him several times as it slowed. When the globe stopped, Vassir's main continent met his gaze. The equatorial nation of Redland stood out from the others on the continent, marked in glaring red.

Kruge grabbed a dagger-like letter opener from his desktop and a plunged it into the globe, straight through Redland.

Lam had not planned on holding their strategy meeting in the middle of Travalia's main street, but that is where the crowds ran, hobbled, and rolled to meet him. Lam and Keneche immediately turned their Highland prisoner over to Jobee, the slow, strong teenager who had pulled him and Lista from their wreck several days before. Jobee's occasional cuff across the head was enough to keep the prisoner in line.

"Who are these men with you, Lam? What is happening?" Aba managed to query above the commotion. The elderly leader spoke for the crowd.

"This is Keneche," Lam explained. "He's a friend who just saved my life."

Keneche's eyes were wide as he looked around at the press of people around him. They were the oddest collection of misfits he had ever seen in his life. Some had missing or misshapen limbs. Some were paralyzed and got about on chairs with wheels or gravity resistors. Some had the childish look of the simple. Others seemed to be blind and wore circlets around their heads, like the attractive woman who was pushing through the crowd to get to Lam.

"Lista!" Lam called to her. "I'm here."

"Do you draw crowds everywhere you go?" Lista asked as she hugged him tightly.

"Believe me, I never try."

Lam laughed and motioned for them all to quiet down. But the hundred or so people who gathered to find out what all the commotion was about were unresponsive to his plea.

Lam finally had to stand on the seat of the skip in hopes of commanding some order. Looking rather rough, he tried to talk above the jabbering of the throng. Keneche stood below, still drying out.

"There is a very serious decision you have to make today," Lam finally began. "Your lives may be in danger—thousands more certainly are. An evil man named Kruge—many of you know who he is—is going to kill a lot of people and become your ruler unless he is stopped." Lam paused until the "boos" subsided. "But you can help—each of you—if you're willing. Do you want to?" Lam might just as well have offered a crowd of children a mountain of candy.

"I'm helping!" Jobee exclaimed with glee; then he decided their prisoner was wiggling too much, so he shook the poor man until he was quiet again.

"This morning is going too fast," Lam complained to Lista later that day. Keneche had already taken his skip and sped off to warn Lassen about the ambush and fill him in on their hastily constructed plans. Lam, along with the whole village, had been busy since then with the preparations for their own little ambush. "The Highland costumes should be finished by this evening," Lam said to Lista as they left the sewing shop.

"The morning has flown, but the preparations are coming along fine," Lista assured Lam.

"The main thing we need done now is our arsenal—after all, we're about to attack an army."

The boardwalk along the river took them to one of the potters' houses. It was a small square wooden building with brightly colored ceramic tile on the front. As Lam and Lista stepped onto the porch, the sounds of the work greeted their ears.

"Welcome to the munitions plant!" Aba greeted Lam and Lista as they walked in. He handed one of the specially designed two-compartment jars to Lam. The potters had been busy making them all day. When the pots cooled after firing, other workers carefully poured a Travalian-made cleaning agent into one compartment, and into the other they poured an antiseptic. Separately, they were just useful compounds, but when mixed together, they generated heat so intense that the mixture burst into flames. Other workers sealed the jars with wax to make sure the chemicals stayed apart.

"We have enough of these to do as much damage as you like," Aba informed Lam and Lista.

"Then let's gather the team," Lam said. "We need to reach the Woodland army before Lassen does."

It wasn't long before the unlikely commando squad had crowded onto the transport and were ready to leave for the Woodland army's camp. Jobee was there, as well as some other strong men and some of the village's technically inclined. Their friends took time out of the projects Lam had given them to wish the team well.

Lam sat on the edge of the transport and prepared to give the signal to move. He felt inadequate to lead the crazy mission— he desperately hoped the Friend would be the real leader. He felt a tap on the knee of the leg that hung over the deck of the transport and turned to see Lista.

"This plan is crazy, you know," said Lista. She knew she wouldn't talk Lam out of it—she just wanted to make sure he was aware of what he was doing.

"Maybe it takes a crazy plan to win an insane war," Lam said matter-of-factly as he sat on the edge of the transport platform and looked down at Lista. "How do you feel about being in charge of the rest of the preparations?"

"That's not my concern. My concern is that you're frustrating, foolish and impossible to figure out." Then she added quietly, "And in case this is the last chance I have to say it, I love you."

Lam took her face gently in his hands.

"You'll have plenty more chances—and I love you, too."

Lista reached up and touched her hands to his and allowed a few painful tears to run down her face.

"Then you'd better come back for me," she said, attempting to be stern. Lam leaned over and kissed the top of her auburn curls. He wished he could leap from the transport and gather her in his arms, but a shout from Jobee reminded him that they were ready and waiting. Lam rose to his feet and ordered the small caravan forward. He turned away from Lista and the village and grasped the handrail that ran around the outside of the platform as they lurched toward their encounter with the army of Woodland.

If Keneche had been a little more experienced driver, he would have been less reckless. But all he could think of was reaching Lassen and his allied forces before they reached Woodland. If he couldn't warn them in time, their plan would fail, and they would face a long, bloody war or a planet dominated by his father and half-brother Kaman. He urged the skip a little faster.

Keneche had been careening around curves and leaping over obstacles in the road since he left the crip village, and he was getting tired from leaning into the controls to avoid one crash after another. But he knew he had to keep up the pace. He nudged the skip a little higher off the ground so he could see farther down the road. There was not much road left.

"Take us over," Keneche told his skip as the road broke up and became a sandy lip of a small canyon. "Whoa!" the yell came out of his throat of its own accord as his skip flew off the edge of the cliff and sailed through the air like a missile from a catapult before it dropped to the canyon floor, leaving Keneche's stomach behind.

"Don't give out now!" he managed to gasp at the gravity resistors. Both his hands were glued white-knuckled to the controls—he wouldn't even let go to grab his helmet as it flew off his head and trailed behind him, rolling down the canyon wall.

The gravity resistors held, and the skip leveled out almost smoothly toward the canyon floor and sped off above the dry riverbed. Keneche pulled his tunic up over his nose to break the wind enough for him to breathe. He allowed one look back and saw the dust roll behind him from his swift passing. His backward glance was brief—he had to be careful not to smash into some sudden turn in the canyon.

He heard them before he saw them. He knew they wouldn't be far—the canyon walls were getting lower as he traveled closer to the pass where he expected to head off Lassen's allied forces. He heard the hum of engines and hundreds of voices that blended into a distant murmur.

When Keneche's skip swept onto the pass, he saw that the crips had already gone by. He stopped his craft to scan the horizon—the glint of the midday sun off the transports assured Keneche that they were not far away. He kicked his skip into action and once again felt the familiar rush of wind in his chapped face. He swung it toward the army and felt his blood surge simultaneously with his skip's engines.

"We're getting very close to our rendezvous with the Woodland army; perhaps it is one of their scouts," suggested Jihrmar. He stood next to Lassen, watching their scouts return with their prize.

"We'll soon find out," Lassen said thoughtfully.

Two Redland skips flanked a third which bore a teenage

driver, now with two shoulder blasters trained on him. When they pulled up next to the command transport, Lassen leaned against the rail and studied the youthful face of their tail.

"Krugeson!" exclaimed Lassen. "What in the civilized galaxy are you doing here?" he demanded, motioning for the guard to help Keneche onto the command transport.

"You've got to stop the march *now*!" was Keneche's breathless reply.

Lam and Jobee lay on their stomachs, hidden by the tall grasses surrounding the Woodland army's camp.

"Are you ready?" Lam whispered to his assistant. Jobee had his eyes shut tight, and had his fingers in his ears when he nodded his head "yes."

Lam told him the explosives wouldn't be loud, but he preferred to be on the safe side. Three blasts sounded from the other side of the camp, followed by shouts of "wildfire!" Several more dull explosions followed, and even from Lam's crouched position, he could see clouds of black smoke billowing up into the once-blue sky.

The commotion moved away from Lam and Jobee as surprised warriors abandoned their posts to defend their camp from the blazes. Lam finally dared to push himself up just above the grass and look up the slight slope to the edge of the Woodland army camp. All he saw were the backs of soldiers as they ran to the fire. Lam knew that when they reached the fire, they would be busy fighting flames, but would find no enemy.

"This is it, Jobee," Lam told his companion. The husky young man took his fingers out of his ears and grinned. Lam was glad Jobee didn't fully understand how dangerous their mission was. "Do you remember what to do?" Jobee nodded. "Tell it back to me one more time."

"I'm supposed to go to the skips and the big guns down there and take these," recited Jobee as he pulled a Redlyn rod cartridge from a sack that hung around his shoulder.

Lam patted Jobee on the back, confident that the young man's strength would be more than enough to dislodge the power supplies. Lam had a different mission, but they stormed the hill together, crouching as they ran.

Lam had scouted the area earlier by climbing a tree outside the camp. Several covered transports looked like they might be carrying water tanks. The water tank by the blazes would be used to fight the fire, so Lam picked out the two closest to him, on the opposite side of the camp from the fires. Lam parted company with Jobee and stole through the long blades of dry grass up to a large covered transport he hoped would hold his target.

He continually watched for Woodland soldiers, but the only Woodlander he glimpsed was a member of his own team. The man wore grass-colored clothes in an attempt at camouflage, and he had flasks of his own slung across his back. Lam watched him dart behind a tent, and he grinned at the thought of those flasks being emptied onto the tent ropes. They carried a much different liquid than Lam's; they contained snapper syrup.

Reaching the transport, Lam looked cautiously around, then flattened himself against the vehicle and listened, deciding it was unguarded at the moment. The distraction they had arranged seemed to be working well. He lifted the camouflaged canvas cover, pushed his flasks onto the platform, then pulled himself up as quickly as he could.

When his eyes adjusted, Lam saw that the transport held a large metal cylinder, sweating with condensation. He strained to open a clasp that held a lid in place over a small opening. The clasp snapped open with a startling clang amplified by the tank. He dropped to his knees and drew his pistol, but soon determined that there was no one to hear his clatter. Satisfied he was alone, Lam tucked his pistol, uncorked one of the flasks and held it up to the opening in the tank. He smiled to himself as the contents gurgled into the water.

Aba told me Travalians take a special pride in their pain reliever, he thought. *Sweet tasting, and potent. Of course, it has its side effects . . .*

The last drop finally splashed into the tank and Lam slung the empty flask around his shoulder. He crept to the flap and slowly drew it back, alert to any sign of soldiers or guards. A sliver of light stabbed into the covered transport and Lam peered cautiously outside—he saw the back of a Woodland soldier. Lam inhaled sharply and let the flap fall shut.

"Who's in there?" the soldier demanded. The point of his shoulder blaster pushed through the flap first. "Identify yourself and come out of there!" the soldier ordered, in a voice whose volume tried to cover up his apprehension. The soldier grabbed the flap and heaved himself up.

Lam looked around him for a quick way to escape and wondered for a brief moment if using his pistol would attract too much attention. The only appropriate weapon he could think of that instant was his empty flask, so he slipped it off his shoulder and prepared to bring it down on the soldier's head—until he realized the empty vessel probably wouldn't even hurt the soldier.

"Why don't you identify yourself?" the guard demanded angrily when he was inside the cover and before his eyes adjusted to the dim light. Lam knew he had to do *something*, so he swung the flask around by the straps and aimed for the guard's ankles. The loose end gained momentum and finally wrapped around one of its target's legs. Lam yanked on the strap, forcing his victim into a precarious dance to keep his balance. When the soldier's head struck the water tank, the cylinder gave a low ring like a bell. Lam hoped no one heard.

"You're going to have a real headache later," Lam whispered to the unconscious man sprawled half under the tank. Lam snatched up the shoulder blaster and slung it across his back. Then he looked out the flap again. This time it was clear, so Lam turned the man's body, jumped down, grabbed him under the armpits and dragged the limp body out of the wagon. Lam knew that if anyone found a body by the water tank, their plans could be ruined.

Lam manuevered his way backward down the hill toward the forest edge, dragging his prize through the grass. His bruised ribs ached from the exertion, but he could not take the risk of leaving the soldier to be discovered.

After a distance too far for Lam's liking, they were finally deep enough into the woods. Lam propped his knocked-out prisoner against a tree stump and explained while he lashed him to it with the flask straps, "Your people will eventually find you. By then it shouldn't matter." Lam tugged on the knots one last time and then trudged through the underbrush for his rendezvous with the rest of his team.

When Lam reached the spot—an intersection of two narrow game trails—Jobee was lowering the last of his captured Redlyn rod cartridges into the hole they had dug in the forest floor to hide the weighty booty. Each one was a rectangle about the length of Lam's forearm and about as thick as his leg. Beside the hole was a pile of dry leaves.

"Hi, Lam," Jobee greeted.

"Not so loud!" Lam warned.

"I got lots of them, see? It took five trips—I counted them myself—the trips, not these things."

"That's wonderful," Lam commended his comrade heartily. "Do you know where the others are?"

"No," Jobee replied somberly. "They'll be okay, won't they?"

Before Lam had a chance to assure him, they heard crashing from the campsite of the woods. Several people were headed their way, breaking sticks noisily under the feet in their haste.

One of the reckless culprits broke into the small clearing followed by several others, breathless from their flight. They were the rest of Lam's team.

"They're right behind us!" the first one gasped.

"How close are they?" Lam demanded.

"Pretty close—I don't think we could make it to our transport."

"You head over that way, and we'll fan out over here," they heard the pursuing soldiers call to each other. One of the soldiers stumbled onto the game trail and looked down the path. Up until then he had been holding his shoulder blaster above the brush, but now he stepped onto the trail and readied it in front of him.

Lam held his breath and listened to the footfalls above his head. Lam originally planned on just storing the stolen Redlyn cartridges in the hole and covering them with cut branches and dry leaves. Now Lam's face was pressed against the dull black units, and the entire crew was covered with leaves, praying that the soldiers would pass by without becoming suspicious.

Lam's hopes slowly faded as the soldier's rustling came closer.

Don't panic, Lam told himself when the footsteps stopped just short of their hole. He pictured the Le-in stone in his pocket and reminded himself that Someone else controlled the soldier's feet.

The soldier's foot stirred the leaves once more and took one step too many.

"What?" the soldier yelped shortly. The leaves in the hole did not support him, and he landed on top of a pile of Redlyn rod cartridges fact-to-face with Lam and the Travalians who had emerged from the leaf pile.

Jobee leaned over to the shocked Woodlander, picked him up, and held him in a bear hug. Lam fished in the leaves and retrieved the captured man's shoulder blaster.

"We're going to have to start a prisoner-of-war camp pretty soon," Lam said. Then he addressed their captive in Common while pointing the blaster at him, "I want you to call to your friends and tell them there's no one in this direction and that you'll meet them back at camp."

The soldier glared defiantly at his captors, all of whom were still buried up to their waists in leaves. He apparently realized Lam would not give away their positions by discharging the weapon. But Jobee tightened his grip and the soldier gasped, his defiant expression turning to panic.

"Let him breathe a little," Lam said after a moment. "Now, sir, I repeat my request." The pale guard gulped air and nodded his agreement. "Smart decision," Lam commended him.

"Where's Bolog?" Lassen demanded of the bowing figure before him. Lassen had jumped off his transport and hurried up to the Woodland militia commander as soon as his troops arrived at the Woodland camp. He tried to look confident and competent, even though he knew they were marching into an ambush. Lassen wished he had his full contingent of Redland Valorians, but he knew Keneche and the eight warriors that went with him had a vital mission.

The commander bowed respectfully.

"He asked me to tell you that pressing matters in Port Cloud have required his presence there, but that he had every confidence in our ability to lead the campaign," the commander replied stiffly.

"I should think he would have enough stomach for the fight," Lassen grunted.

"Would your troops like refreshment? We have fresh Woodland spring water. We had to use some of it on fires earlier this afternoon, but there should be plenty for all of us."

Lassen's parched throat begged to accept the offer, but he knew better after Keneche's briefing.

"No! No, thank you, we have our own. Our plan is still to march at nightfall?"

"Yes, sir."

"Then we should order the troops to rest while they can. I think you and I, along with my commander, the Seaward and Sundor commanders, and our squad leaders should take advantage of the time and review our strategy."

"Of course. I'll have the command tent readied for us."

Lassen returned the Woodland commander's salute and rejoined Jihrmar at the command transport. Lassen stood on the ground, looked up to Jihrmar on the deck of the transport and nodded gravely.

The sun ignited the horizon with an amber glow as it settled behind the hills. The Woodland watchman leaned against a tree on the perimeter of the camp and breathed deeply of the wood scents that spiced the air. He always enjoyed this quiet time of day when it became cooler—and today was especially quiet since the entire camp was under orders to rest for the march and battle this evening. Of course, they knew it would be a brief battle— as soon as they crossed over into Highland, they would be ambushed by the Highland militia, and Woodland would also turn on their supposed allies. But for the sake of Redland, Seaward, and Sundor, they rested. No soldier he knew was going to complain about a chance to nap, anyway.

The guard glanced at his partner sitting on a fallen tree trunk not far from him, sipping water and leaning on his shoulder blaster. The water looked good, and he was about to unstop his flask when he heard the snap in back of him. He turned around leisurely, expecting to see a comrade or a small animal; instead, he found himself staring into the dark faces of Sundor soldiers—fierce men, wearing long knives sheathed in leather straps that crossed their bare chests. Each held an activated shoulder blaster aimed at the Woodland guards.

"Gorn!" he shouted his partner's name. There was no reply. The savage looks in the brown Sundorian eyes told him to put down his weapon, so he carefully laid his shoulder blaster on the grass and looked back at Gorn. His partner was sprawled out comfortably on the grass snoring, still clutching his now-empty water flask.

In the camp, teams of Redland, Seaward, and Sundor soldiers poured out of their tents and spread across the slumbering camp. The surprised Woodland guards on the evening watch surrendered cooperatively and were bound and gagged; now the allies moved into the rest of the camp, quietly lifting the flaps of Woodland sleeping tents with their Redlyn pistols drawn and ready.

In the command tent, Lassen and the other commanders were just finishing their lengthy review of strategy. About twenty smartly uniformed men sat at a round wooden table in the stuffy tent. Dusk had just encroached upon the camp, but no one had taken time to raise any lights. The twilight concealed the anxiety present on every face there.

"Well, this sounds very, very good," said Lassen, rising to his feet with a stretch.

"Yes," agreed the Woodland commander. "The plan should give us both surprise and tactitcal advantages over Highland. Is there anything else we need to cover?"

Lassen stood and thought for a moment.

"Just one more matter," Lassen finally said casually. He tipped his head in an exaggerated nod, and all the squad leaders from Redland, Seaward, and Sundor leaped to their feet and drew their pistols on their Woodland counterparts. "That other matter is, 'Surrender your weapons,' " Lassen answered.

"Slime eaters!" yelled one of the Woodland squad leaders as he slammed his pistol on the table. The Woodland commander, a heavyset, older man with as many medals as gray hairs, sighed heavily in a pretense of resignation and gingerly removed his weapon and set it on the table. As he did so, he discreetly pressed a button on his wrist unit.

Piercing sirens sounded throughout the camp in response to the Woodland commander's signal, and he allowed himself a smug smile, confident that his well-prepared troops, now alerted, would turn the tables in their favor once more.

The slumbering Woodlanders on the side of camp near Lassen's tents woke with a jump at the alarm, but when they opened their eyes, they found enemy pistols greeting them. Lassen's counter-ambush had not reached the far side of camp, however. There soldiers sprang from their bedrolls and grabbed their shoulder blasters.

"Get up!" one soldier ordered his tent mates as he strapped on his gold-visored helmet. There was no response. "Get up, bashampta breath!" he shouted urgently, jabbing one of them with the butt of his blaster. The only response was an annoyed snore. He shook his head in disgust and unstopped his full canteen. "Maybe a face full of cold water will give you ambition," he told his comrades.

Outside the tent, syrup from the tent ropes collected in pools at the stakes. Flies had been feasting on the sticky substance all afternoon, but as the already-set sun yielded its last spray of color, a clicking sound emanated from the grass. The sound was familiar to Woodland, a sound most woodlanders avoided: night snappers.

A pincer the size of a man's big toe clamped onto a tent rope. Two spherical eyes set on the top of two moving stalks joined its claw at the rope's level, and the mouth—a round orifice with five sharp teeth pointing toward the center—began to chew on the sweet hemp. Around the tent, more night snappers climbed out of their holes and scurried on their six legs toward the tents, clicking.

The creatures became frenzied over the syrup, and their sectioned bodies scrambled over each other to get to the sweet prize. The lucky ones that made it to the ropes tore into it with their teeth, and in moments, the high-tension cables began to snap, flinging night snappers everywhere. The tent poles toppled and the canvas collapsed on top of the soldiers within.

Outside, the battle had begun. The Woodland soldiers who had not drunk the drugged water, and who managed to crawl out from their collapsing tents, and who were not already prisoners, ran to find defensible positions from which to make a stand. The only cover on the grassy hill was provided by the Woodland vehicles. The Woodland soldiers dived behind them as Redlyn bolts sang past them and burned into the ground at their heels. The Woodlanders answered the fire from Lassen's troops, who had made it only halfway through the camp before the sirens sounded. Lassen's men and their allies scrambled behind the tents and dropped to the ground where they attempted to force the Woodlanders' surrender.

The Woodlanders began to mount the skips they had been hiding behind. They were provided by Highland and plated with a blaster-resistant polished armor. They switched on the skips and prepared to move against their attackers, using the powerful Redlyn blasters mounted on the front of each. Behind them, transports with destructive ener-bolt throwers also began to hum to life. The engines hummed, but the vehicles did not rise from the ground.

Cursing and kicking could not make up for the lack of Redlyn rod power packs. Jobee had managed to render most of the weapons impotent. Outgunned and commanderless, the Woodlanders one by one threw down their shoulder blasters and fell face down on the ground with their arms behind their heads in surrender.

Lassen stood in the middle of the camp and watched his militiamen and their allies round up the Woodland prisoners.

Jihrmar stood next to him and smiled.

"We won," Lassen's cousin and commander declared cheerfully.

"We've won a small battle," Lassen agreed. "But we have at least one more to fight, and perhaps the most important one is out of our hands—it depends on a teenage boy and an alien."

"I don't deny that we have a hard fight in front of us, but for the sake of the troops you'd better show a little more enthusiasm," said Jihrmar sternly. "You are asking them to risk their lives."

"That's exactly why I lack enthusiasm, Cousin."

Chapter Seventeen

The river water grew thick and dark like molten metal as the sun yielded the sky to Vassir's moon. A large log bobbed in the current just off the shore—an ordinary-looking log, except that it floated upstream.

Two men stood with Lista on the Snowy River's bank and proudly watched their boat motor upstream. One of them set his bulky power chisel on the grass and motioned to his deaf co-worker.

"It looks like they float," he repeated out loud for Lista's sake. A second log boat was still lashed to a tree on the shore. Keneche was the last to step into it, and his face revealed the effort he poured into keeping the craft from tipping. When he was safely seated, Keneche waved to the craftsmen on the bank.

"I have to confess that I am a bit amazed at the skill I've seen here in Travalia," he called up to them. The one who could hear modestly shrugged his shoulders.

"I'm glad you're amazed," Lista called down to Keneche. "You're doing the right thing in opposing your Father."

"More than I ever suspected," Keneche agreed.

Keneche settled in and looked at the three other men in the boat with them. They looked so ordinary dressed in Highland street clothes, but he knew they were far from ordinary. Their shiny black armor lay stacked in a corner of the sewing shop. These Redland Valorians did not look as fierce when separated from their armor, but their disciplined reserve was intriguing. The fur-lined clothes could not completely conceal their powerful physiques, and not all of them had hair enough to cover the shiny finders each wore around his head.

Keneche unconsciously attempted their casual attitude. But

152

he could not push from his mind that the handful of them were on their way to overthrow a dictator—one who happened to be his father.

When Lista heard the Travalian boat builders casting off their creations, she called down to Keneche one more time, "When you see Lam, tell him that I'm praying to the Friend for him—and tell him I miss him."

The torchlight highlighted Lassen's stern features as he briefed his squadron leaders near his command transport.

"Until the complete victory is ours, I won't trust these Woodlanders as far as I can carry water in my bare hands," stressed Lassen. "I want them to know plainly that if anyone tries to escape or harm any of us, we will swiftly execute all their squadron leaders—as well the offending soldier."

"Are those your orders, sir?" asked one squadron leader in charge of guarding the prisoners.

Lassen hesitated for a moment, then looked to Jihrmar. Jihrmar tipped his head discreetly to nod yes.

"Those are your orders," Lassen solemnly replied. "But I pray the gods, if they care, that we won't have to do that. Highland will be bitter enough. You and your men do everything you can to prevent such a tragedy. You'll be on your own, the twelve other squads will be marching with me into Highland. We'll see if a counter-ambush can work twice in the same night."

Behind them, foot soldiers finished dragging the last of the supplies onto the command transport. As the last crate dropped to the deck, the gravity resistors activated with a crack and emitted a low hum. In other parts of the dimly lit camp, the Woodland skips and guns received spare Redlyn rod packs so Lassen's allied troops could turn them against their makers.

The squadron leaders hurried to their troops and transports. The transports, each capable of carrying fifty troops and a few skips, were rumbling to life and rising from the ground. Gunners on the transports swiveled the captured Woodland ener-bolt throwers in their turrets to make sure they responded well to their new owners.

"I wonder if Keneche is right and his father kept his Valorians to guard the government center," Lassen said.

"It does not matter either way," returned Jihrmar, somewhat annoyed at having to encourage Lassen. "They are just Vassirians like you and me."

"Valorians have saved my life before, remember? They can take lives just as easily."

The command transport hovered just above the ground behind Lassen in the light. He turned and grasped the handrails of its ladder and climbed to the deck.

"I know we've been over it a hundred times," Lassen grunted as he pulled himself up. "But I'd like to review our new strategy one more time. We will approach from the northwest instead of the southwest as they are expecting. Our aerial fighters will hit first, targeting their vehicles and major guns—this should draw the Highlanders' attention and fire away from us. While they are thus occupied, we'll strike and keep them scattered and defensive as long as possible."

"That's the plan," Jihrmar confirmed as he swung himself up to the transport platform next to Lassen. The transport rose higher and began to move as the others did, headed for what they hoped would be the last battle of the war.

Lassen looked up at the clouds gathering above them, blocking out the stars. The wind felt cooler on his skin, foreshadowing a storm just as his troops' preparations foreshadowed the battle. "If we're not victors, we'll never see that sun rise."

Lam buried his hands in the pockets of his tunic to help fend off the chill. Dew was already collecting on the long blades of grass that hid him from all directions except the river. He kept his eyes on the river for the boats he hoped would be coming for him, and he kept his ears open for night snappers. There was no sign of either.

Lam decided to give up his vigil and sit on the bank. *Maybe the Source is giving me some time to rest*, he mused.

Lam smelled the tangy sweet smell of decaying vegetation from the forest floor as well as the exotic scent of the night flowers blooming on the sandy bank. Long white spikes from the blooms seemed to glow with a light of their own and lured insects into the spiraling center where the plant would digest them. He had parted company with the rest of his team earlier that evening. They had returned to Travalia, and Lam waited for his next mission. He barely had time to flatten the grass in his new spot before he heard the gentle lapping of water against the bows of boats. Lam quietly slipped behind a stand of reeds where he could safely study the newcomers. The night as well as the reeds hid Lam, and he couldn't see anything in the river except some hints of movement. He made a clicking noise with his tongue and listened. Moments later the hollow splash of a pebble hitting the water disturbed the quiet. Two more splashes followed, and then it was quiet again.

"Keneche, I'm over here!" Lam called out quietly.

As he stepped into one of the log boats, Keneche said, "Lista misses you." Lam's ears burned in the cool night air. "Thanks," he returned gruffly.

"I've been anxious to hear how your raid on the Woodland army camp went," Keneche continued. He stood with one foot in the boat and one in the water to steady the craft while Lam tried to make it in.

"I'll tell you when I'm inside this thing. Getting into this is like trying to stand on a ball." Lam finally managed to get both feet in and sit down so that his weight helped add the necessary ballast.

"I'm pleased to report," Lam said to Keneche, now working on re-boarding as well, "that Woodland won't be ambushing anyone tonight."

Keneche grunted his approval, still concentrating on his balance.

"That's not my major concern. I'm worried about what happens when we reach the government center," Keneche answered. "But we'll be to the border soon—probably reach the government center a little before dawn."

Lam nodded to show that he had heard, although it was hard for Keneche to see him in the deepening darkness. Soon Elna would be completely set and they would have to rely on other means to pick their way through the darkness.

The crew was quiet for a while after they resumed their northbound trek.

"Do you serve the same deity as Altua?" Keneche asked Lam, mostly just to distract his mind from dwelling on the hundreds of things that could go wrong with this scheme.

"Yes." Lam's voice was hesitant, apprehensive. "But not very well," he confessed, "or very consistently."

"Do you think he's with us on this?"

"I haven't paid as much attention as I should have, to tell you the truth," Lam admitted. "If I were he I wouldn't bother— I haven't even talked to him much lately. But yes, he's with us."

Lam glanced back at the three men behind him in the log boats. They seemed relaxed and unconcerned about the danger they would be facing. It was hard for Lam to tell because of the darkness, but it looked as though at least one chin rested against a chest in slumber. He knew all that could change in an instant, though. Keneche told him about the Valorians, and that he hoped Lassen would choose them from his own army for this particular mission.

Lam turned again to the swirling water that parted before their log and stared in thought.

"Ken, what do you know about Valorians?" Lam asked Keneche quietly, still looking ahead.

"What do you want to know?"

"How are they trained?"

"Some of the discipline is secret. But I can tell you that it takes years of building physical strength and agility, heightening the senses and learning the discipline."

"I wish I had that kind of discipline behind me—we're not exactly going to play in a solar ball tournament, you know."

"I know how you feel. If I get any more nervous, I'll jump in the river and head for the woods."

The two of them were quiet for a long time after that. They watched the water splash past the boat, and the dimly lit trees on the bank marched past them in a uniform procession. Each wave and each bough they left behind reminded them that they were getting steadily closer to their feared encounter.

Lam felt a tap on his shoulder.

"We're getting close to the Highland border, I believe," said Keneche. "There is a small stretch of rapids we'll have to pole over, but there's a section near the bank that was cleared when barges used to ship ore from the Highland mountains to the other parts of the continent."

"Good, I think," Lam acknowledged. "Pass the word back that as soon as we're over the rapids, we take cover and slow the motors so we won't attract any attention."

I shouldn't fear, Lam upbraided himself. *I should be calm like the Thunder Fighters—after all, I destroyed the Dominion.* Immediately Lam flushed, angry at himself for imagining he had that much to do with the defeat of the Dominion. *It was by the Power— the Power I have hardly called on since I left Tsu. Is it too late to start again?*

"Do you hear it?" Keneche said—although he spoke quietly, he crashed into Lam's thoughts. When Lam did not immediately answer, Keneche explained as if to a slow student, "The sound of the water over the rapids—do you hear it?" Keneche was already pulling out his pole, made to look like a limb protruding from the trunk of a fallen tree.

Before Lam could answer or get his own pole, the metal keel of the craft struck rock with a dull clank and wedged in the stone. The stern of the boat began to swing with the current and collided with the grassy bank beside them. Already prone to tipping, the upset rocked the clumsy craft dangerously—it was built for camouflage, not maneuverability. An image of himself and their weapons drenched and floundering on the rocks flashed through Lam's mind.

Lam immediately yanked out his pole, swung it over the head and plunged it into the water. The Valorians' poles were already there, steading them and launching them forward over the rocks. A quick glance behind him saw that the other boats were following—roughly and noisily, but surely.

Calmer water was not far ahead, and as soon as he felt the last rock scrape against the keel, Lam heard the motors slow to silent running. The rustling around him also told him that the company was taking cover beneath the bark-covered canvas that stretched over the narrow opening in the tops of the log boats.

Lam did the same and became engulfed in a stuffy darkness deeper than the night outside.

Lam listened to the steady breathing of the men cramped in the boat with him. He listened to the water lap past them outside, and he listened to his own racing heart. He had no idea how fast or slow time was passing inside his cylindrical cell—all he knew was that it seemed like forever before Keneche took a chance to whisper,

"We should be into Highland by now."

"Shh!" snapped Lam. Keneche's was not the only voice he thought he heard. Muffled voices from the riverbank confirmed his suspicion.

"Boarder patrols," sighed Keneche under his breath. "Perhaps they won't notice us," he offered wishfully. Any hope that they would float by unseen was dashed at the sound of the guards discussing the strange phenomenon of logs floating upstream. Lam could not understand their Highland speech, but it sounded as if they intended to investigate. Lam's heart jumped as one of them rapped on the log with the butt of a shoulder blaster.

"I don't think we should wait for them to open us up like a can of vegetables," Lam told the Valorians and Keneche. "We might as well satisfy their curiosity," said the Valorian closest to Lam, almost in a casual tone.

Without warning, the Valorians rolled to one side and tipped the boat so the opening faced the shore, and in the same movement, they leaped out and onto the shore, barely touching the water. Lam would have marveled at their nonverbal coordination, but he was busy pulling his face out of the water where he had spilled out during the Valorians' maneuver.

Glaring lights flooded the bank, blinding the men who had been sitting in the total darkness of an enclosed boat.

The Valorians struck fast, and the shocked Highland boarder patrol did not recover quickly enough to keep their blasters from being snatched out of their hands. There were only three of them, and two were quickly pinned to the ground. The third managed to pull himself together and dart for his skip. Two Valorians ran after him, although the Highlander was on his skip and lifting off the ground before they could reach him.

The pinned Highlanders watched with terror as their comrade attempted escape. The Valorians in the other boats were sitting up and seemed to be thoroughly entertained by the whole drama. Lam and Keneche had dragged themselves from the water and watched, too, Lam clenching his fists in frustration at not having been able to help.

The Valorians in pursuit of the escaping skip gestured to each other briefly, and when they reached the spot beneath the skip, one squatted down and cupped his hands, the other fell back and then ran toward him. The power in their muscles, hidden by their fur-lined Highland clothes, revealed itself as together they launched the runner into the air. The acrobatic Valorian flew upward, grabbed the runners of the skip and began to pull himself up.

The Highland guard felt his craft lose balance and looked down to see hands on his runners. The Highlander raised his boot to crush the Thunder Fighter's fingers, but as he lowered it, the Thunder Fighter grabbed it and pulled, using the Highlander's own momentum against him. The Highlander lost his balance and slid off his seat. He grabbed at anything he could to remain on his now out-of-control craft, and in the process knocked the helmet from his head. It fell to the brush below, and after one sharp blow from the Thunder Fighter's forearm, the Highlander followed.

"I'm sure there was a com-link in that helmet," Keneche warned Lam. "I hope he didn't have a chance to alert the government center."

"We don't need any more welcomes like this," Lam agreed.

Battle-ready Highland soldiers paced anxiously at their posts. Some stood and gazed into the darkness of the woods looking for movement they knew probably wasn't there, and others entertained themselves by throwing different size sticks into a circle drawn in the dirt and wagering on the results.

Chairman Kruge had put his son Kaman in charge of the Highland militia during the rearming. He was particularly anxious as he sat in a camouflaged lean-to that served as a command post and waited for a sign of the enemy. He had expected to hear a report from his scouts long ago saying the allied armies were approaching and that it was time to carry out their co-ambush with the Woodlanders. But no word came. Since they were under transmission silence unless they had news, he could only assume that something was holding up the enemy. At least he hoped that was the reason they were still waiting—this was the most critical campaign of his career, and probably his last if he failed.

He sighed and leaned back in his folding chair. He looked up and saw that the clouds which had begun to form earlier that evening had completely shrouded the stars. In fact, the breeze was so much cooler, he decided with disgust that it was about to rain. The low rumble of distant thunder confirmed his prediction. A brighter flash filled the sky above him, immediately followed by a deafening crack that seemed to echo forever across the countryside. The sound of rain hitting the dry leaves of the woods floor alerted him to rainfall's initial drops.

"Tell the troops to maintain their positions no matter how wet they get," Kaman ordered a nearby aide. Another flash and thunder peal shook the woods, and he looked up to identify the direction the lightning was most active. As he stared, he noticed that the thunder echoes were not dying down but getting louder. He stepped out from beneath his shelter to get a better look at the horizon. To his horror, the roar was from the engines of three approaching fighter ships, their black outlines only visible in the lightning flashes.

The ships screamed overhead and launched a brief but well-aimed volley of red bolts at their position. The commander heard his troops shouting in panic and scrambling for cover. The large transport-based guns swung into service and laced the sky above them with red slashes of deadly energy of their own, but the fighters had split formation and sped off in different directions. Several of their largest guns were already seriously damaged, and the commander stood in near-shock as he watched flames leaping from his transports.

Kaman pulled himself together and ran to the center of camp and shouted orders at the dashing soldiers around him.

"Man the ener-bolt thrower! Form flanks around your standards!" he cried. But before they could rally from the first attack, the fighters screamed toward them again, now approaching from three different directions. The turret of the Highland ener-bolt thrower that was still operational swiveled toward the oncoming ships and a brilliant blast erupted from the gun. The hasty attempt missed the ships and instead engulfed a stand of trees which disintegrated into ashes from the attack.

The soldiers began to leave their former positions and formed flanks as Kaman had ordered. He suspected that the enemy would be attacking from the ground next. They did. But before the allied armies fired a shot and revealed their positions, trees began to fall on the Highland army camp. Their attempt at defensive flanking shattered as the Highland soldiers ran to avoid the giant hazards. Metal crunched and glass crushed noisily as the timbers landed on the camp. Next came the blaster fire, raining on them from all directions. The Highlanders scattered in panic.

"This is V One to V squadron; do you note the situation?" The voice was calm as it transmitted via com-link from a triangle-shaped craft with swept-back wings to others like it flying in formation behind it.

"Yes, V One," each aerocraft reported in turn. The crew of the craft wore dark red, highly polished armor and helmets with gold visors. They were Kruge's Valorians, sent to monitor the success of the ambush. What they witnessed was a disaster.

"Engage enemy fighters," the lead pilot ordered.

Chapter Eighteen

Keneche looked nervously at the sky.

"There's rain coming our way," Keneche predicted.

"Water I can handle," Lam said with a grunt. He and the others were heaving their log boats onto the shore near the mouth of the port city's storm sewer system, its formidible grate thick with moss.

"Are you related to River Rainers?" Keneche replied. Lam shot a glance at Keneche and wondered what he meant. Then he looked at the storm sewer and realized that if the rains were too heavy, they would be swept away as they traveled its damp interior, drowned and deposited in the river with the rest of the city's refuse.

"Pray for a drought," Lam urged. He handed Keneche a branch he had just cut from a tree and turned to cut another to help hide their boats.

"I wonder how Lassen's doing," Keneche said worriedly. "There should be quite a battle going on by now." Lam stopped for a moment and listened. Low rumblings drifted to his ears on the cool breeze—they could have been explosions, or they could have been thunder.

"He's probably wondering about *us*," Lam said.

A squatting Thunder Fighter took a white bottle from a bag on the sand beside him and squirted a potent corrosive onto the metal grate over the sewer mouth. The moss smoke from the heat generated by the chemicals and the grate itself hissed and crackled. Two Valorians, their motion in harmony, stepped back a few paces and then ran toward the grillwork, leaping into the air, and sailing toward the weakened grate. Just the sound of the impact made Lam's bones hurt, and he watched in amazement as the men reached in and pulled out the heavy grill which had just collapsed from their kick.

One of the Valorians buckled for a moment—under the weight of the metal, Lam thought, until he drew near enough to see them in the darkness. Acid dripped from the jagged stubs protruding from the conduit and burned through the Valorian's clothes, causing him to stumble with the sudden pain. He and his partner tossed aside their load, and the injured warrior walked calmly to the river and washed off his shoulder. Lam marveled at the discipline a warrior Valorian exercised to keep his pain in such control; he could fight undaunted until his heart stopped.

The small band wasted no time in filing into the conduit, forsaking fresh air and dry boots for the duration of their journey underground. Lam was last in, and he wasted no time scraping his knuckles on the rough surface inside the black conduit.

"I think it's safe to turn on some light in here," Lam called up to Keneche. No one answered him, but a dim light flickered on that at least kept him from tripping over his own feet and landing face-down in the small stream of stale water already flowing through the system.

They hadn't traveled far, but it seemed like ages to Lam. He was almost sorry he had asked for light. There was nothing to see but section after section of gray tunnel. And it was definitely not designed for travel. Lam's back ached from bending over and his legs felt as though they might give up at any time, tired of supporting his hunched body, tired of walking on a curved floor that made his feet turn inward.

His thoughts turned in on him in the same way the walls did. Lam had nothing else to do during the monotonous journey except think—he thought about the Valorians. They were strong, quiet, and seemingly undisturbed by the peril ahead. The chill of his envy matched that of his soaked boots as he compared his own sloppy thoughts and fears to the disciplined resolve of the Valorians. And as long as he was accusing himself, he added rebellion to his personal list of recent failures.

I am a follower of the Way of Tsu, protected forever by the Power of the Source and the Friend, Lam scolded himself. *But lately I think*

I've made a better enemy than ally to him. I've got to take control of myself.

"Be careful when you round this corner," Keneche warned the band following him. "There's some junk in the way hung up on the corner joint."

The junk Keneche referred to was the rusting remains of the security drone. Lam apprehensively wondered how many of those things wandered around these tunnels, but he was grateful for any distraction from the endless gray tunnel walls.

Kaman Krugeson looked into the sky and let the rain pour down his face. His boots were partly sunk in the softening ground beneath them, and the insects flooded from their leafy covers and swarmed around the heads of all the soldiers.

"What do you want with me?" Kaman raged. "Are you making sport of us, Redlander? Why don't you just shoot us all?"

Lightning flashed in Kaman's eyes, reflecting the brilliant discharges in the night sky above him. Through the thunder, the allied fighters made another pass, torching the sky with their own fire. Highland soldiers ran from the fighters' path, jumping for whatever cover they could find as their vehicles and large guns continued to explode in the attack. Kaman gazed at the devastation in despair until a new sound pulled his attention skyward.

A fleet of sleek swept-back winged aerocraft roared into the battle and engaged the three Doomen fighters Redland had converted. Hope again seeped into Kaman's drained body, and he risked climbing onto one of the few remaining transports.

"Look up! Help has arrived!" Kaman exulted into his voice-caster. Only the closest to him could hear, but he trusted word would spread through the squad commanders. "Rally at your standards and heed your commanders." He repeated his orders several times and then jumped to safer ground to attempt contacting his squad leaders by com-link.

"I see them too," the third allied fighter pilot said flatly into his com-link. The allied ships were piloted by Redland Valorians and co-piloted by Lassen's best technics. Advanced circuitry in the Valorians' black helmets overlayed an electronic image of sensor readings on the inside of the gold visors. The location, size, distance, and makeup of the ships were displayed by graphic representations over a green dot grid, and information about the enemy ships and their own ship danced before the pilot's eyes. The technics saw the same information on screens in their control panel. The ship then responded to the pilot's eye movements as well as the manual commands he gave.

"Defensive formation four," the Redland Valorian leader ordered calmly, and the three ships split apart and prepared for a deadly aerial battle.

"Marking enemy aerocraft at point 03," the offensive allied fighter in the position relayed.

"Fire on mark," said the fighter leader. Red lances flashed in the viewing ports of the fighters, but they missed the slender craft that pursued two of their fighters. The silver aerocraft broke formation to cover wider territory and choose their own marks among the tiny fleet of allied fighters.

"Fighter two requesting cover."

"Stand by."

The allied fighters had the superior ships, but they were outnumbered, and the small Highland aerocraft made difficult targets.

"Fighter three confirming strike on enemy craft."

Redland's fighter three watched his Redlyn bolts score a direct hit on an aerocraft fuselage and then he pulled up sharply. Even as he relayed news of his success, he witnessed the Highland retaliation. A Highland aerocraft broke away unexpectedly from the game of tag it had been playing and took advantage of a fighter preoccupied with two other aerocraft. A storm of red fire erupted from the aerocraft and tore into the Redland fighter.

The armor tiles from the fighter peeled away where the aerocraft delivered its blow, and the damage to the gravity resistors sent it spiraling downward.

The face of the Valorian pilot revealed fierce determination as he pulled on the controls and tried to rein in his wild craft. The technic stumbled from his seat to make repairs, but the force of the fall pinned him to the inside of the fuselage, rendering him helpless to correct any damage.

The disciplined Valorians in the remaining Redland fighters refused to waste time watching their comrades crash. They redoubled their defensive and saw that the damaged Highland aerocraft had left the battle and was limping back to Wyntir.

"We've got to get out of here!" Lam shouted to Keneche above the roaring water, approaching waist deep. Keneche looked back at Lam and the Valorians as they used the rough round walls to push themselves against the current. He turned again and looked down the tunnel. His hair was matted against his head with sweat and sewer water. His eyes had a desperate look that revealed his desire to press on.

"But we're so close," Keneche pleaded.

"If we get any closer we'll need gills," Lam retorted. Keneche struggled to decide what to do.

"All right. We can get to the street if we double back about a section and a half. But the street will be patrolled, and even these Highland costumes aren't much of a disguise when they're soaking wet."

Lam had almost forgotten what reasonably fresh air smelled like. With his elbows, he pulled himself out of the sewer through a hole in the street. The rain had slowed to a tolerable drizzle mixed with a few snowflakes, certainly nothing compared to the flood they had just fought.

The Valorians scattered to scout for enemy patrols, but Lam and Keneche had to pause to stretch their backs and shake out their legs cramped from the cold water. "Now I know what it must feel like to be hatched from an egg," Lam complained.

"Except that once you've made it out, it's supposed to be brighter," Keneche added, looking to the sky. The clouds covered Elna and the stars, and the city observed the strict lights-out order.

"It's so dark it seems dead," Lam commented.

"In a way it is," Keneche said darkly. "My father's taking away the things that make us alive."

"Well, Ken, let's do something about that." Lam touched

the finder, half hidden by wet hair, and activated it.

Each man knew what to do next. Coded responses vibrated into his inner ear and told him the location and nature of all the objects around him. He had not been able to practice much, and so couldn't understand most of the data that the instrument flooded his mind with, but he could at least keep from walking into buildings and tripping on steps. The others did the same and struck off toward the government center.

The night was half over by the time Keneche dared to whisper that the next building would be the government center. They didn't need the finders to tell them that—the government center was fairly well lit, and they could see the soft glow of the light against the drizzle a couple of blocks before they saw the building itself.

"They've stopped," Lam whispered to Keneche. The silhouette of the fighter blended with the black outline of the building beside them.

"Just beyond the corner we should be able to see the center," Keneche explained. When he caught up to the eight Thunder Fighters, Lam saw that Keneche was right. Even the cold drizzle didn't dampen the spectacle the Highland Government Center made. The building was not ornate or graceful, but rather square, and massive like the mountain into which it was built. The center structure was four stories tall, and one corner was made of glass. The smaller wings attached were also square and made of the same red-tinted stone. Relay posts surrounded the grounds and marked the location of the ener-fence. Crackling flashes where insects crossed the fence proved that it was activated.

"There should be one guard at the gate to the ener-fence. Then there is a standing guard at the main entrance and a roving guard on those paths cut into the mountain above the center. There is also one guard on each floor inside."

Without speaking, two Valorians began to make their way toward the gatehouse.

The lights that shone on the building glared off the wet pavement. Against the reflections of the government center in the pools on the pavement, the two Valorians appeared only as dark silhouettes. Lam watched them dart from a statue to a raised bed of flowers for cover until they had stolen their way to the gatehouse that guarded the entrance. The gatehouse was built of the same reddish stone and had room for two guards to watch activities around the fence. However, the nights were usually uneventful, and this time of year they were long, so to stay awake they often wagered on games of sticks. The game that night was especially absorbing.

One Valorian crouched beside the gatehouse beneath the windows and reached under his tunic to remove a pellet and a sling. He placed the pellet in the sling's pocket and swung it beside him until it hummed. The pellet flung from the pocket into the wall of the government center with a short crack and a flash. It was just enough to get the guard's attention, and they hastily picked up their pistols and hurried from the gatehouse. Lam watched the Valorians jump the guards, and through the stillness, he heard necks break.

The almost casual ease with which the Valorians killed the guards shocked Lam. Again the faces of his own victims flashed back to him. They were, for the most part, soldiers or ship crew who knew they might have to die for the Dominion. But Lam was a pirate, and he had no right to take those lives.

Lam wished he had the luxury of privacy and time to talk these things over with the Friend. Instead, he closed his eyes in the Vassirian darkness and the cold Highland rain, and silently poured out his heart. He knew the Friend was already aware of his past and the lawless life he led, but admitting it to himself in front of the Friend seemed to take away the pain of each one.

"I know the Valorians are unthinking, just doing well what they are trained to do," Lam whispered desperately to Keneche who seemed pleased at their progress. "Is this what will happen to Kruge when we catch him? Are we just going to break his neck or pierce him through with a Redlyn bolt?"

Keneche's smile faded from his face as he considered Lam's words.

"Vengeance must be ours—who else is going to care?" Keneche demanded. "Do you think the gods care? If they did, they would not have let things go so far; they would have stopped my father from ever—from ever harming anyone. When Altua came to confront my father, I heard some of what he said about the Source and the Power—I even prayed to them, but did it do any good?"

Lam grasped the lad firmly by the shoulders and looked deeply into his eyes.

"I believe that the Power sent me here to save the lives of innocent people—I don't believe he sent me to take lives. I admit there were times when I thought the Source abandoned us, but now I see that he's been guiding us all along. Think about it! He brought us together, he led you to Altua, we found out about the plot, he saved our lives and helped us warn the allied troops before they reached Woodland. He saved us from drowning, and he provided us with transportation, a way to navigate in complete darkness—all this and more. Do you really think he doesn't care?"

Keneche's eyes burned for a moment as he resisted the notion that their success until now had been due to anyone but themselves and motivated by anything other than vengeance. Then he remembered his vow in the archives—to give credit to Altua's God. He hung his head and shook it slowly. It was not necessary for Lam to give further examples of coincidences too good to be chance.

"Defend yourselves," Lam said to the remaining Valorians, more calmly now. "But we will take Kruge and Brakan alive— they have a solar system to answer to, and it should be up to the people to decide how they should pay—not us." The silent men around him nodded in agreement.

Some light from the yard filtered through the windows into the hallway, but it took their finders for Lam and the others to distinguish the obstacles from the shadows. Keneche had led them through a less obvious entryway on the side of the government center building, apparently undetected. The youth explained curtly that he had contacted his allies at the government center from Travalia and arranged to have the entrance left open. The real challenge would come when they reached the entry plaza.

"The stairs should be on our right," whispered Keneche when the hall merged into the plaza.

On the wall to their left were paneled wooden doors that led outside. They were nearly two stories tall and carried Lam's gaze upward to the balconies that overlooked the entry plaza. Over the railings of the balconies hung the Vassirian banners— red with the hexagram and globes, a reminder of whose fortress they were assaulting.

At least the doors are closed and unguarded, Lam noted. Then he looked up at the massive stone staircase which wound its way up to the next floor. The side of the building which supported the staircase was nearly all glass, and the yard lights flooded through and banished all the cover they had hoped would allow them to escape the notice of roving guards.

"We'll just have to take a chance," Lam said. The Valorians had already come to the same conclusion and had pushed past Keneche to begin their silent ascent. Lam switched pistol hands and flexed the fingers that had nervously gripped his weapon too tightly. He shook his hand and regripped his weapon before he looked both ways and struck off after Keneche and the Valorians.

Chapter Nineteen

The stairs seemed endless, and Lam was afraid his panting from the exertion would be enough to alert a guard. With each breath, his ribs punished him, but he ignored them and diligently scanned the railing of the floor above, hoping there would be nothing to see. Somehow he knew hope was unrealistic, so he remained tense and watchful.

Lam saw that a couple of Valorians had already made it to the wide landing that marked the halfway point of their upward journey. According to Keneche, his father's study was just down the hall on the floor above them, and that is where he expected to find the Chairman, brooding over his plans, which by now he might know were falling apart. Lam saw the Valorians on the landing drop to the floor and then he looked up and saw the glint of a military-style pistol swinging from the side of a passing guard. The guard had apparently not yet noticed the group.

Lam and the remaining Valorians moved quickly to the stone railing that afforded minimal cover from the eyes of the guard. Perhaps he would not be able to distinguish their forms from the railing posts unless he looked at them directly. Keneche lunged for cover, and his foot, still damp from the flooded sewer, slipped on the polished stone step. He grabbed for the banister, and his Redlyn pistol clattered noisily down the stairs.

The guard hurried to the railing, working to unhook his own pistol from his belt. Lam saw that the Valorians from the landing were running, still unnoticed, but without cover. Lam decided he'd better distract the guard and give the Valorians a chance to make the top of the flight.

"Hey, ugly! Are they paying you to sit up there and look cross-eyed?" Lam shouted in his native tongue of Entar.

"Who's there?" the guard responded in Highland. But that was all he could do before a Valorian hand from behind clamped over his mouth. In an instant, he was disarmed and bound.

No one knew if the guard's shout gave them away. Lam and the others hurried up the steps, hoping to reach the second floor where massive square pillars provided some cover. They made it as far as the landing.

"Look out!" shouted Lam when he saw two more center guards running down the hall toward the rail where their comrade was captured. Lam's warning was slower than the Valorians who leaped at their new threat. The first guard received a drop kick in the ribs and the other ducked behind a stone pillar to shoot from a safer distance. The Valorians stood in the open and blasted at the pillar, knocking out the guard's defense chip by chip. The Valorians were so good at anticipating the guard's moves that whenever he ducked from behind his pillar to shoot, they jumped out of the way as if the Redlyn bolts were simply airborne seeds floating gently toward them in the breeze.

By then, the other six Valorians had neared the top of the flight. The cross fire lulled momentarily when light flooded the hallway and the stairs. Floodlights from walls glared down on them, part of the security system screaming to life with sirens blaring.

"Hardly the sneak attack we planned!" Lam shouted to Keneche standing beside him on the landing.

"It's all my fault!" Keneche cried as he ran down the stairs.

"No, wait a minute," Lam said. "We wouldn't have gotten this far if it weren't for you. Where are you going?"

"I'm getting my gun and I'm going up there to help."

Lam looked worriedly after their impulsive guide, and then back up to the balcony. The Valorians had taken cover from a volley of Redlyn bolts that sliced through the air on the second floor. More guards had shown up, and they were not going to be taken by surprise.

Chairman Kruge, looking more gaunt than usual, reclined in his seat behind his stone table, watching the stairway battle on a monitor. He tapped his fingers against his lips in a sort of calm that comes from being overwhelmed. Brakan sat opposite Kruge, also watching the monitor.

"It's very interesting that this should happen," Kruge said darkly. Brakan turned to look at his leader. Kruge continued, "You persuaded me to allow Lam Laeo to escape, and then you let him escape again, only this time with the complete outline of our strategy." Kruge was beginning to flush as he spoke, and Brakan's hand would have been trembling if it had not been resting on Kruge's stone desk. "Who else is there to blame but you for this disaster?"

"This is what happens when you put a boy barely out of adolescence in charge. And that traitor Keneche is your son too—and didn't I say not to leave those fighters on Neece?—" Brakan began to blurt in defense, but a buzzer on Kruge's desk sounded, and the Chairman sat forward to switch on his com-link.

"Valorian aerocraft two returned to port," he heard the pilot announce.

"Report," Kruge ordered.

"Since our last communication, our squad destroyed one enemy fighter ship. The army appears slightly outnumbered, but there are some major weapons advantages still intact."

"I understand. Report immediately to the government center. We are under attack and our guards are only holding them back. And bring the Valorian from the fighter docked at the port—we need him here more than the army does." Kruge watched the monitor as he spoke. "The attackers are dressed in street clothes, but the way they move, I believe they are Valorians, probably from Redland—we'll need your help against them."

"Understood," the pilot acknowledged.

Kruge glared at Brakan for a moment and then back at the monitor. The Chairman had a wild look in his eyes, his gray hair looked like the waves of a storm, and his skin was ashen except for the anger that showed like a rash on his neck and cheeks.

"We could all be dead tomorrow," Kruge whispered faintly. Then after a moment determination returned to his features. "When we take care of these minor difficulties, there will be some people who will have to explain a few things to me personally—and I have a feeling I won't be satisfied with their answers."

Above the burning and embattled woods of Highland, the wearied pilots continued their struggle against the Highland aerocraft.

"Pull up that wing," the allied squadron leader ordered. "You're getting sloppy!"

The pilot obeyed and pulled up but over-compensated, exposing its belly to the approaching Highland aerocraft. The squadron leader watched the electronic representations of the scene on the inside of his visor—the amber outlines of his partner ship out of control, the three converging Highland aerocraft represented by smaller electronic drawings falling into a direct firing line. The outline ships began to flash, signaling immediate danger.

"Hide your belly! I'll come to cover!" the squadron leader yelled into his com-link. But even as he spoke, as his technic ran his hands across the panels to make sure the ship was responding at its peak, the three aerocraft loosed a trio of deadly Redlyn bolts at the vulnerable ship. One of the enemy bolts just grazed the tip of its wing. The other hit the hull near the most curved surface and glanced off, doing minimal damage. But the last one scored a direct hit on its upturned belly, touching off an explosion that rocked the allied ship and sent it spiraling downward.

"We lost a grav-resistor," the crippled fighter's pilot reported. "Instituting emergency stabilizing procedures." The squadron leader watched as two diamond-shaped wings snapped out from the ship's hull. Orange flames flared from the engines as the pilot attempted to fight the ship into control now that it had some lift properties. Slowly it stopped spinning, but it was still plunging toward a collision with the trees below.

An unsteady voice yelled over the shaking of the plummeting ship, "By the gods, I see things flying below us—lights or birds! Can you pick them up? What are they?"

The squadron leader examined the amber outlines in his visor, but they revealed only one ship—a ship that was about to crash.

"Negative. Can you control the ship? You must pull out of that dive."

"Negative, the controls are not responding—ahh!" The voice of the troubled fighter pilot trailed into a surprised cry as the ship did a loop and leveled out. The pilot hit his helmet against the side of the ship, but the straps kept him seated.

"Report!" the squadron leader commanded. His own attention was diverted to evading the approaching aerocraft, so he didn't see what happened next. By the time he could check the wide angle view in his visor, his partner seemed to be under control.

"Ship is leveling out and responding to controls," the pilot answered almost as if nothing had happened. "I don't know what happened, but we'll make it down. Sorry we can't stay for the games."

"Report to commander Jihrmar and we'll see you in the victory parade. Wait a minute—you have an admirer."

"I see it," the pilot said. A Highland aerocraft was pursuing the damaged allied ship like a bird of prey hounding a wounded animal—and it was narrowing the gap. "I think I'll see how it likes tight spaces," the pursued fighter reported.

The dark form of the modified Doomen fighter pulled out of the course that would have led to an open space where it could land and instead swung into the steep-sided canyon. The canyon walls loomed around them, lighted only by lightning strikes. The Valorian pilot navigated the treacherous course by the lines projected inside his visor, and hoped the aerocraft pursuing him dared to follow. It did.

The dark water and silent rocks hurled past the speeding vehicles, the roar of their engines echoing off the usually lonely cliffs. Startled birds dove from their ledges and flew circles in the wake of the passing ships. Then the Redlyn bolts began to pierce the air, adding their deadly flashes to the lightning strikes. The river below them, swelled in a flash flood caused by the heavy rains, washed down a hundred hills to the canyon floor, and the allied ship seemed to brush the tops of the waves as it passed. The Highland ship stayed higher and attempted to follow its intended victim.

"Keep that last grav-resistor steady," the Valorian pilot said to his technic through his com-link. "We don't have any room for wavering."

"The quarters are too close," the technic complained.

"It's close for the aerocraft too—I'm sure it takes all their discipline to follow us."

A bend in the river and a turn of the walls faced them suddenly. The allied ship deftly banked and straightened to its new course. The Highland aerocraft also banked, but as it did, its left wing dipped into the raging river water. The river had crested unexpectedly and clutched the aerocraft in the torrent. The craft found itself facing the rock walls of the cliff as it spun. Its tail hit first and crumpled as the fuselage collided with the unyielding stone of the bank. Flames erupted, and the explosion loosened rock above the burning wreckage, burying it without ceremony. The allied ship pulled up out of the canyon and landed safely on the plateau above it.

The squadron leader did not allow himself the luxury of gloating. Instead, he diverted his attention to the enemy fleet he now faced alone. His technic sat in his seat and fussed over the sensitive controls and mechanisms that kept them from joining the wrecks below.

"What is our strategy?" the technic asked into his com-link.

"Our contingency orders are to keep the enemy occupied."

"That shouldn't be too hard—the trick will be staying alive while we do it."

Lassen's men had been wedging their way into the enemy position like roots breaking up soil. In theory, Lassen was to monitor the troops with Jihrmar from the command transport and advise them in safety, but both Lassen and Jihrmar stood behind reflective shields on the deck of their transport and returned enemy fire. The downpour battered against the two, and their once-impressive uniforms dripped from their aching limbs.

"Well, you suggested we fight the Highlanders at close range so they couldn't use their heavy weapons," Jihrmar quipped between shots. "If we get any closer I'll be able to count their teeth."

"Let's not get any closer!" Lassen shouted above the din of the screaming Redlyn bolts and the roar of the thunderstorm.

"How's the air battle going?"

"Those cursed Highland aerocraft are just little sub-orbitals with no gravity resistors—our fighters could wipe them out in moments if it weren't for those satellites Kruge put up with those deadly things up there, our fighters have to stay low to the ground or they'll be shot down! But we have our own problems down here."

"If we continue these nonlethal scatter tactics much longer, we'll be surrounded and we'll have to start defending ourselves."

"What choice do we have? A bloody victory will be a short-lived one—I'm sure of that!"

Keneche raced down the stairs, eyes fixed on the dull gleam of his Redlyn pistol at the foot of the stairs. Above him the battle raged, and he longed to join it. His foot finally landed on the bottom step, and he reached down to pick up his prize. While still reaching for his weapon, two dark red boots appeared in his line of vision. A wave of dread swept over him and he barely forced himself to look up. He stared into the golden visor of a Highland Valorian. He wore a dark red armor, and looked poised for a fight. Behind him, another Valorian followed, drawing his shoulder blaster from his back as he strode.

Keneche knew better than to attempt out-drawing them or fighting them. He would not have dared beat his fist against the red armor if he thought it would do any good, anyway. Instead, he turned and ran. And screamed.

Lam turned from the battle above him when he heard Keneche's cry. His heart sank when he saw the reason. Perhaps they could handle the guards, but now they were surrounded—guards above them, Highland Valorians below. Maybe it was the shock of seeing the enemy Valorians, but Lam began to feel detached and distant, as though he were only a bystander.

He came to find an elderly statesman and found himself in a life-and-death struggle to preserve hundreds of lives in a village for crippled people. Now he found himself fighting to overthrow the government.

If I was chosen for all this, then why am I so poorly equipped and nearly crippled because of these ribs? Lam reasoned with himself in the strange quietness of his own thoughts. *Why don't I possess a discipline like the Valorians?*

Discipline. The word hung on his thoughts. "Discipline" is the word Hud used when he taught him about following the Power. Lam's discipline came through study on Tsu, hundreds of hours in intense concentration and reaching out to the Power inwardly. It was the discipline of yielding his own will to the will of the greatest power in the universe.

Lam sank to one knee on the stairs, broken by the impending disaster he was powerless to prevent.

"This is my discipline!" Lam shouted to the ceiling. "I give up! If you can't use me, pierce me through with a Redlyn bolt now!"

Keneche scrambled up the stairs and collapsed onto the landing, grabbing Lam's arm as he fell.

"Highland Valorians!" Keneche gasped, barely able to speak between gulps of air. "What are we going to do?"

Lam looked down at the frightened boy and saw a reflection of his own fear. Lam decided to take a chance and trust the Source he thought he believed in all along. Lam's scowl softened.

"It'll be all right, Ken," Lam said reassuringly. He pointed to the metal circlet on his head—just like the one Keneche wore. "The Source gave us a way to find our way through the darkness. What we need is more darkness."

"I know where the junction box for the floodlights is," said Keneche, his panic easing. "If I could only get outside."

"Good. I'll cover while you shoot your way out of here."

"You expect me to shoot my way through Valorians?"

"No," Lam answered. "Shoot through that." He pointed to the window and then Lam dropped behind the twist in the banister to occupy the enemy Valorians while Keneche leveled his antique Redlyn pistol at the glass wall and pulled the activator. Nothing. Keneche slammed the weapon against his hand in what had become a reflex. Still no Redlyn fire.

"God!" urged Lam.

Keneche glanced back at Lam, busy with the red-armored

Valorians, and then looked back to the window.

"In the name of the God of Altua and Lam!" he said, and aimed one more time. After a red flash, the glass in the window shattered into melted fragments. Before he ran to the gaping gash he had made in the glass, Keneche called to Lam, "When I'm through knocking out the floodlights, I'm going to the space-port. Remember those government-center friends I told you about? They're meeting me there along with someone Lassen should be very happy to see."

Before Lam could reply, his young partner was on the narrow ledge beneath the windows.

Just like Ken to have his own schemes going, even in the middle of a battle he helped start, Lam thought. He shrugged and then turned his fire to the chandelier above the stairs. On the third shot, Lam managed to sever the fixture from the ceiling and it fell in a shower of sparks and glass. The Highland Valorians jumped out of the way in plenty of time, but the Redland Valorians, taking Lam's lead, each marked their own light and knocked it out. In a few loud moments, the entire area plunged into darkness.

Chapter Twenty

Brakan, you have a chance to make up for your bumbling," said Kruge, pulling open the door to a small cabinet behind his table.

"They're on the stairs," Brakan said weakly. He stared at the battle on the monitor in Kruge's study, suddenly gone dark except for the flashes from the weapons' fire. "They're just outside the study—I can hear them."

"We have the fools well outnumbered here and in the Highland woods as well. You heard the last report—they're down to one fighter!"

"Maybe you can fool the Council, and the army, and maybe you can even fool yourself, but I know we're outnumbered—I know we're losing." Brakan faced Kruge, his face red with humiliation.

"Take this and come with me—I will personally see these slime-eaters pay for the damage they've done. They'll repair the scars in this building with their bare hands, and then I'll watch them each die." Kruge snatched up a bulky, military-style Redlyn pistol from the cabinet and hurled it at Brakan. Brakan covered his face with his arms. The pistol hit his forearm and clattered to the floor. He glared at Kruge, then bent to pick up the weapon. It weighed down his hands as he turned it over, feeling the power it held. He gripped it by the handle and pressed his thumb against the barrel end. It activated with a whine.

"Now get out there, and remember who's destined to rule!" Kruge ordered.

"Destiny follows its own course, Chairman," Brakan said. "I don't know why I thought we could change it."

"Shut up!"

"If nothing else, you taught me how to shoot from the hip,"

said Brakan as he raised the pistol and leveled it at Chairman Kruge.

"Brakan, we are going to rule—think of it! You'll have more than a ball of rock to govern—you can have a whole nation. Vassir will rise up to destroy you on its way to greatness even if you shoot me—it's destiny, and we were simply riding on its crest. Riches—they can be yours, too—"

Lam ran the rest of the way up the stairs, using his finder to locate the last step and the Redland Valorians. He couldn't locate a single Highland guard—each hid behind the stone pillars unable to see to aim their weapons. All they could do was strain to hear some sound that would give them a target. Then the finder, vibrating information into Lam's skull, told him that the Redland Valorians were silently stalking the guards.

They'll soon have them, Lam thought. *I had best get out of their way; I'm not going to be much use in hand-to-hand combat,* he realized, rubbing his aching side. Lam slipped as quietly as he could behind the marauders and pressed himself against the cold stone of the hallway. In spite of Lam's caution, his boot clicked against the wall. He dropped to the floor knowing he had just given the guards a target, and a red bolt tore a gash in the wall above his head where he had been standing. When the stone chips had settled, Lam continued to creep down the hall—this time without his boots. *They're just too noisy,* he thought. So he left them by the site of his close call.

The two Highland Thunder Fighters had silently crept to the top of the stairs and waited in the darkness, their senses straining to fix on their unseen enemy. The flash from the bolt aimed at Lam gave them a brief image that burned into their eyes. They knew that their Redlyn counterparts would scramble and realign themselves in some other effective encroachment, but they decided Lam was a potential prize.

"See what you can do here. I'm going to take the small one across the hall," one Highland Valorian told his comrade through their helmet com-links.

Lam reviewed in his mind the directions to Kruge's study Keneche had given them all earlier. He knew it should be just down the hall—if he could keep from advertising his presence too loudly, he might make it. The finder told him how far it was to the end of the hall and he stole toward his goal as quickly as he dared.

"There they are!" a Highland guard shouted, shielding his eyes from the sudden light spilling from the stairway. One of the guards had managed to make it to the panel that controlled the display lights in the hallway, and although they were rather dim, the illumination seemed blinding after the total darkness. As if the light switch had also turned on the battle again, the allied commandos rushed on their enemies instantly. A storm of Redlyn fire filled the hall, and the frightening battle cries from the Valorians multiplied the din of the fight.

By the time Lam reached the door, his chest hurt from the exertion of his dash down the hall. Lam pushed on the handle and found, not surprisingly, that it was locked. He stepped back a pace and leveled his pistol at the barrier. A couple of moments and several well-aimed shots later, Lam was able to kick what was left of the door in. Pistol raised and activated, he stalked the room to the far side where another door stood ajar. As he neared it, he could almost feel Kruge's presence. He could hear nothing, but light poured through the crack into the dark lobby Lam traversed. Even above the din of battle, Lam could hear his own heartbeat. The closer he got to the second room, Kruge's study, the more he wished the Redland Valorians were next to him.

The door yielded with one kick, and Lam leaped into the room, his weapon raised and ready to shoot.

"Brakan!" Lam exclaimed. "Where's Kruge?" he demanded, threatening the moon-base commander with his pistol.

"Don't shoot, please," Brakan pleaded as he bent over slowly and laid his weapon on the floor.

"Where's Kruge?" Lam repeated angrily. Brakan pointed to a body heaped on the floor. Lam stared in disbelief at the body—it certainly looked like Kruge.

"I shot him," Brakan confessed. "You owe me for this, Laeo. It's all over now, and it's because of me—I assured your victory today."

Lam continued to stare at the pathetic form. He was angry

because Kruge would not have to stand trial or face public condemnation. He was relieved that it was all over, but could hardly believe it was true. Lam simply stood and tried to collect his thoughts.

"Traitor!" hissed a voice from the door. Lam and Brakan swung around to find the red-armored terror point a glowing pistol-tip in their direction. Lam lifted his own weapon, but before he could warn the fighter to drop his weapon, the Highland Valorian's pistol discharged a bolt that instantly found its mark and bit into Brakan, sending him staggering backward. His eyes bulged, and he choked on his own cry of pain. He sank, still clutching his wounded belly, to the floor beneath the monitors.

The Valorian carefully laid his weapon at his feet, raised his hands and announced to Lam, "Part of our philosophy is a well-timed surrender," the Valorian said calmly, his voice distorted by his helmet.

"It's long overdue," Lam answered. "Get on the com-link and tell your comrades in the hall what time it is."

The shuttle appeared like a comet in the night sky above the battlefield on the Highland border. Landing lights cast a brilliant path through the rain and flooded the war-scarred ground beneath it. Most of the weapons stilled as the warriors shielded their eyes and stared wonderingly at the vessel that dared to land in the middle of their hostilities.

Even before the landing legs of the golden shuttle finished settling into the soft earth, the hatch hissed open, spilling intense white light from its gaping mouth. A moment later a figure appeared in the hatch. The back lighting scattered in pulsating rays off the gleaming golden armor that clad the figure. The armor covered his entire frame, and a lowered golden visor descended from the helmet, as did golden chain mail that cascaded onto his broad shoulders. A white fur cape with tufts of black hung behind him and was clasped around his neck with a golden chain.

Lassen abandoned his caution and ran in the open to the shuttle and up the gangway.

"Whatever god brought you here, I thank him," Lassen said, grasping the hand of the figure standing in the doorway.

"If my new friend's story is correct, that god's name is the Source and the Power," Cruzan, the Valorian Master, replied. Keneche and some other somber men dressed as Highland government-center guards or servants joined Cruzan. This was the group that was conspiring against Chairman Kruge long before Lassen joined the struggle. Now they hoped to end the conflict by bringing the most universally respected leader on Vassir.

"Please, come with me." Lassen turned and strode back to the command platform with Cruzan. The Valorian Master was a fourth again as tall as Lassen, and his aged face, though half covered by a golden visor, revealed inner strength and determination. His armored gloves chinked against the handrail as he pulled himself onto the platform where Jihrmar waited. Jihrmar immediately recognized the legendary man whom Valorians throughout the continent respected no matter what their allegiance. After bowing reverently before Cruzan, he grasped a com-link pickup.

"Jihrmar to all squad leaders. Cease fire immediately," he ordered and then handed the pickup to Cruzan. Lassen also held the pickup for the voicecaster in front of Cruzan so that the Valorian's voice would be broadcast to everyone.

"Fellow Highlanders, I ask you to cease hostilities in the name of the discipline," Cruzan's voice boomed. Each word rang with authority and conveyed the same intensity he wore on his face. "You will not be defeated, but you will be the victors, choosing your own destiny rather than being destroyed by the wild notions of a dead madman."

Lassen smiled broadly as he considered the effect the man's words must be having.

"I, Cruzan, have just learned that Chairman Kruge is dead— killed by Brakan, who is also now dead. Your cause no longer exists."

Kaman heard the words cutting through the mist, and they bit into him sharply. He lowered the sight-amplifier from his eyes—it was Cruzan, all right. The shoulder blaster slipped from his weakened grip and fell into the mud at his feet. He walked back to his shelter and sat on his chair, which had seen little use that night, and tried to comprehend the news of his father's death. Cruzan's words rolled off like water from a dry sponge.

He sat and watched the soldiers around him discussing what to do among themselves. A squadron leader finally walked up to Kaman and waited to be acknowledged. Kaman never looked up. "Sir, do you have any orders?" Kaman never responded. "If I might be so bold, an official surrender would be in order. The troops are already laying down their arms." Kaman just blankly sat and watched Highland's aerocraft land, their vertical thrusters blasting craters in the soft ground. Then he watched the feared Valorians drop from the cockpits of the aerocraft and walk up to the battle line. He knew the armored warriors would have no question of allegiance. Cruzan was like a god to the Valorians. Kaman reviewed his losses: The new Vassir was gone—the Master Planet a mutilated dream. His father was gone, and even if the new rulers of Vassir had mercy on him, he could not imagine what life would be like without his father's support and guidance.

"Shoot me!" Kaman ordered the squad leader who still stood in his shelter, waiting for direction from Kaman.

"Certainly not, sir," the officer refused, a look of shock dominating his young face. Kaman rose and staggered toward the soldier.

"Do it now!" Kaman cried. When the squad leader refused again, Kaman grabbed at the man's pistol. The officer drew back the hand that held it and Kaman fell into the mud, breaking into sobs.

Lista reached out toward the face her finder told her was there, leaning against the tree on the riverbank. He had been standing on the riverbank, silently watching the moonlit eddies and currents in the Snowy River. He had grown to feel a sort of kinship with the river. The river was not the only part of Vassir he had grown close to. As he watched the water, he fingered the delicate gold ring he had cherished since his adolescence on Entar. Before knowing the Friend, the ring used to calm him and help him think when he was nervous. He'd rub it between his fingers and think about his home on Entar. It always made him sad, but he cherished the feelings it gave him.

This time the ring had a different effect.

"It seems like a nice evening, Lam. Tell me what it looks like."

Lam smiled and took her hand.

"It's still, and there are so many stars in the sky, it looks as though some artist exaggerated the scene for effect. Elna is hanging just above the horizon and looks twice as big as usual."

Lista stood with Lam and tried to imagine what it must look like.

"You've been so reclusive, you probably haven't heard the news today."

"There's more news? It would be nice if nothing would happen for a while."

Lista laughed gently and continued.

"The Council—the original one—named Cruzan, Keneche's grandfather, as acting chairman. Most of us thought Lassen would do it, but he said the Queen of Sundor invited his family to her estate for the winter and he's taking her up on it. Keneche, by the way, is quite the hero—he's already left for Redlyn to train with the Valorians there."

"I imagine the original Council is short at least one member," Lam remarked.

"You're right. The Valorians still haven't caught up with Bolog, the Woodland delegate, but I doubt that he's the type who can live off the land."

Lam laughed even though he was trying hard to maintain his pensive mood.

"The Council also commissioned a Travalian artist to sculpt a monument in honor of the team you took into the Woodland militia camp. They're going to put it in the government center courtyard in Highland. They are also working on a new agreement between Vassir and Neece that will give Neece much more say in their own governing, which should ease tensions all around."

"We should try to reach Me'Ben," Lam interjected as Lista reminded him of Neece.

"I'm sure we'll be in touch with him," Lista assured him. "The Council also officially thanked Altua and granted him Vassirian citizenship. They even offered him an office at the government center and two personal servants."

"Somehow I can't imagine a Tsuian sitting in an office."

"I think I did hear that he turned it down—but he's taking on the servants as his assistants, at least that's what I've heard."

The two of them stood on the bank and listened to the quietly churning water and the cooing night birds.

"Lam Laeo," Lista scolded her companion. "Why are you still so moody after all the news, and after the tremendous success we had?"

"Didn't you get the message I left with Aba for you?"

"You mean the one telling about Entar and how you became a pirate after it was destroyed? Yes, I did, and I'm furious with you for not telling me sooner. What kind of a woman do you think I am? A while ago I told you that I love you. I love who you are right now, and your past can't change that, no matter how bad it was."

Lam smiled, but continued his quiet direct questioning.

"Do you believe in the Source?" he asked quietly.

"I think most of us are beginning to after all that has happened. As for me, I asked him one thing—to protect you. And he did. And it's a good thing someone looks out for you. I'm still not sure how he did it, but you're here. Yes, I believe in the Source."

"I have to go back to Tsu," Lam said after rewarding Lista's confession with a hug. "I have certain obligations there. They're rebuilding, and I'm still studying there. My studies will mean much more after the lessons I've lived here. I don't want to leave you, but you have a home here, and Tsu is a very long way away."

Lista wrapped her arms gently around Lam's bandaged chest, and he stroked her hair as she silently enjoyed his warmth.

"I do have a home here, but I'm willing to consider other offers," she finally said with a smile.

Lam held her tight and lowered his head to kiss her cheek and stroke her blushing skin with his hand. She reached up and held his hand, feeling its gentleness and strength as he caressed her face.

"How about an offer of marriage?" he whispered. Lam took Lista's hand and gently pressed his cherished ring in her palm.

"Worth considering," Lista said breathlessly.

"I've been considering it a long time," Lam laughed nervously. "If I ever had a doubt that's what I wanted, I don't tonight. You look so beautiful—we've been through some painful times, but looking at you makes them all blur." He paused and bent to kiss her trembling lips. "I love you, and I want you with me always. I want us to get married. So, how's that for an offer?"

"Maybe it's because I'm as crazy as you are, but I can't imagine a better one."

Lam gently cupped Lista's radiant face in his hands as he drank in her beauty. He could hardly believe that she loved him—enough to wander halfway across the civilized galaxy with him. He pulled her close and decided that it felt so good, he'd stay there until sunrise—night snappers or not.

Altua stood beside Aba's humming grav-resistor chair in the middle of the small crowd that had gathered to watch Lam and Lista leave Vassir. Lassen had found time before his trip to Sundor to have Starjumper brought back from Elna and serviced. The ship gleamed from a new coat of paint and her engines were powered with a full supply of Redlyn from Lassen's own mine.

"It was such a lovely ceremony," Aba commented to Altua as they watched the couple board their ship, waving. "Somehow it seemed like such a special union—they seemed so completely united and happy."

"That is because they are bound together in the Power," Altua explained as he waved at Lam and Lista. "Ah, they are so young."

"I wonder how old they will be when they reach Tsu," mused Aba.

"They told you of their plan to take the long way back, too, eh? It's smart—they'll have little peace when they first reach Tsu. I know those people well—they'll not want for company, that is certain."

"I hope they have a long, quiet life together," said Aba, leaning back in his chair as Starjumper's hatch locked the newlyweds into seclusion.

Starjumper's engines began to glow, and it lifted from the pad—slowly at first, then picking up speed. When it hovered high above their heads, the engines flared and Starjumper bore the couple skyward.

"A quiet life is one thing I doubt they will enjoy," Altua said with amusement in his voice. "You will see for yourself how it is soon enough—those who serve the Source, no matter how they might crave a dull life, are rarely allowed to rest for long."